THE WINDS OF CHANCE

THE WINDS OF CHANCE

Lynne Collins

Chivers Press · Thorndike Press
Bath, England   Thorndike, Maine USA

This Large Print edition is published by Chivers Press, England, and by Thorndike Press, USA.

Published in 2000 in the U.K. by arrangement with the author.

Published in 2000 in the U.S. by arrangement with Juliet Burton Literary Agency.

U.K. Hardcover ISBN 0–7540–4243–X (Chivers Large Print)
U.K. Softcover ISBN 0–7540–4244–8 (Camden Large Print)
U.S. Softcover ISBN 0–7862–2807–5 (General Series Edition)

The text of this Large Print edition is unabridged.
Other aspects of the book may vary from the original edition.

Set in 16 pt. New Times Roman.

Printed in Great Britain on acid-free paper.

British Library Cataloguing in Publication Data available

Library of Congress Cataloging-in-Publication Data

Collins, Lynne.
    The winds of chance / Lynne Collins.
      p.   cm.
    ISBN 0–7862–2807–5 (lg. print : sc : alk. paper)
    1. Large type books.   I. Title.
    PR6057.R3268 W56   2000
    813'.54—dc21   00–044690

CHAPTER ONE

Howard Blair came down the steps from the block of offices, whistling softly. He was a tall, heavily-built man in his early forties.

Another man, younger and slimmer in build, turned a corner and Howard hailed him quickly. 'Oh, there you are, Johnny! I was just coming to find you.'

Johnny Greer stopped short. He wore the grey slacks and yellow sweater which was the uniform wear for the male staff of Blair Holiday Camp. The girls also wore yellow sweaters, but on sunny days they combined them with brief white shorts or tennis skirts. On colder days they wore neat grey skirts. The sweaters were all the same shade, manufactured by the same firm, loose-fitting and warm enough to combat the chilly wind that sometimes swept across the low-lying countryside from the sea.

'I want you to take the camp car and meet the two-thirty, Johnny,' Howard said easily. 'I'm expecting my new secretary. Her name's Gail Anson.'

Johnny nodded. 'Right you are!' He grinned. He was a good-looking young man with fair hair that was not quite blond but which would brighten in the sunshine that summer. His friendly blue eyes and easy smile

1

made him very popular with staff and campers alike: his looks and warm personality had helped him to get the job as Assistant Organizer and Howard Blair was very pleased with Johnny's devotion to his work. He had taken the young man on without any former experience only two seasons before and now he was beginning his third season. It was a pretty safe bet that many old campers returning to Blair for another holiday would look around anxiously for some sign that Johnny was still at the camp and greet him with warmth and pleasure. Now his blue eyes twinkled. 'So it's true that Susan isn't coming back this year?'

Howard nodded. 'Quite true.'

'Tony will be relieved,' Johnny said lightly.

'Gail should be a pleasant addition to the staff, Johnny,' Howard said evenly. 'She's my niece.'

Johnny raised his eyebrows. 'Oh, I see.'

'Don't spread that information around,' Howard interjected quickly. 'Gail doesn't want it generally known, and I quite understand her point of view. She will work as hard as anyone else and there won't be any differential treatment.'

'Two-thirty at Combleigh, did you say?' Johnny glanced at his watch. 'I'll be on my way.' He turned away, then swung round quickly on his heel. 'How shall I know her, Howard?' he asked swiftly.

Howard grinned suddenly. 'I don't think you'll miss her,' he replied. 'She's small and dark and very pretty.'

The two men parted and went their separate ways.

Howard moved on towards the big Main Building which housed the ballroom, the dining hall, two large games rooms, a nursery for children, a quiet room where the campers could read, write letters, play cards or watch television in the evenings; it also housed a large cafeteria which was very popular with the campers, despite the three excellent meals which they had every day. They always seemed ready for a hot or cold drink, a cake or a sandwich.

As usual, the camp was fully booked for the coming season which opened in three weeks' time. Final arrangements were in hand for the welfare, comfort and entertainment of the campers who came from all parts of England. Its main advantage was its situation on the South Coast which could claim the maximum sunshine for that part of England: the private beach with golden sands and safe sea-bathing was a very popular feature of the camp; so were the brick chalets with their colourful, modern appearance, hot and cold running water, and very comfortable furnishings.

Nothing had been overlooked to ensure the full enjoyment of any holiday-maker who chose Blair Holiday Camp.

Howard entered the Main Building. His footsteps echoed through the empty building as he crossed the ballroom floor and he smiled to himself with inner satisfaction as he thought that in a few weeks' time the place would swarm with people. The whole atmosphere would be charged with general happiness and light-hearted fun.

At the side of the dais in the ballroom was a door which led into a small office where Tony Sheppard, the Chief Organizer, drew up plans and lists and ran the general entertainment affairs, assisted by Johnny.

Very few of the permanent staff had arrived as yet: the two organizers were needed for conferences to decide the plans for the season—carefully going over the activities of the previous summer, deciding which had been popular with the campers and could be used again, and which had not been whole-heartedly approved by the campers. At Blair, the holiday-makers ruled: their wishes, their enjoyment and their tastes were always the first consideration of Howard Blair and his staff.

The kitchen staff and the waitresses would not arrive until a few days before the season opened: neither would the girls who cared for the children so that parents could really enjoy their holiday without having to keep an anxious eye on their infants; local women were employed as chalet-cleaners and other

4

cleaning tasks also came their way.

A holiday camp of the size of Blair needed a great number of staff. Their private chalets were erected in a separate part of the grounds with their own washing and ironing facilities, baths and showers, and relaxation rooms. They were allowed to use the ballroom, the swimming-pool and most of the other facilities that had been introduced for the campers, but it was a strict rule of the camp that they must not mix socially with the holiday-makers. Naturally enough, this was a difficult rule to enforce, for some of the waitresses were pretty and personable and young men on holiday were not likely to ignore their charms.

Howard opened the small office door and put his head inside. Tony glanced up from the lists he was compiling.

'Hallo,' he said. 'Did you want me?'

Howard entered the room and closed the door behind him. He leaned against the wall, folding his arms across his chest. Indicating the lists on the table, he asked: 'Are those the staff lists?'

Tony nodded. 'It's a devil of a job trying to sort out the off-duty periods,' he said ruefully. 'I'm always clashing with something important. I'm just trying to arrange it for the umpteenth time.' He groaned in mock despair, threw down his pencil and tilted his chair back. He picked up a packet of cigarettes which lay on the desk and opened them. 'Have one?' he invited, offering the packet to Howard.

Howard took a cigarette and produced matches from his pocket. When both men had lighted up, he said: 'I've another member of the staff for your list, Tony. My niece. She's arriving this afternoon.'

Tony raised his eyebrows in almost an identical gesture as that of Johnny Greer. 'Your niece?' he repeated. 'A member of the staff?'

Howard nodded. 'That's what I said. Gail wants a job—I want a secretary. She's to be treated just like the other girls, Tony—no favours, mind!'

'But she'll be living at the bungalow?'

'No. You'll have to find her accommodation even if it means sharing with one of the other girls.'

Tony whistled soundlessly. 'I'll do what I can,' he said at last. 'But it will mean some reshuffling.'

Howard smiled. 'I could have waited until the season started and then introduced her to the camp,' he reminded Tony. 'That would have meant a more difficult reshuffle.' He took a long pull at his cigarette and then stood looking down at the glowing end while he exhaled smoke from his lips and nostrils. 'Let me see—what about that red-headed girl in reception? Is she coming back this year?'

'Ann Mathers?' asked Tony. 'Yes—do you want me to arrange for your niece to share a chalet with her?'

'She seemed a very nice girl,' Howard said lightly.

Tony nodded. 'She's a friendly kid—I imagine your niece will need someone like Ann to show her the ropes!'

'She knows nothing about the camp. I doubt if she's ever been to a holiday camp in her life,' Howard said with a grin. 'Her father is inclined to think rather badly of them. I never did like Hubert Anson—either before he married my sister or after!' He did not notice the sudden flicker in Tony's eyes, and it would have meant nothing to him if he had. He dropped his cigarette to the floor and ground his heel on the butt. 'Gail will soon settle down,' he said confidently. 'She's very much like her mother—an adaptable, easily-pleased type.' He touched Tony's shoulder with a careless hand. 'Give her a helping hand, would you— to, begin with, anyway?'

Tony nodded. 'Sure,' he said mechanically. He glanced meaningly at the papers before him and stubbed his cigarette in an ashtray.

'Okay, I'm going,' Howard assured him with a light laugh. 'I'll leave you to your struggles.' He paused just before he closed the door behind him. 'I expect Gail could be very useful with that sort of thing,' he added. 'You must get her to give you a hand.'

'She'll have enough to do,' Tony protested.

There was a mischievous gleam in Howard's

eyes as he said slowly: 'Susan was always very busy—but she found time to do odd jobs for you.'

'It served as an excuse to hang around me,' Tony said curtly.

When Howard had gone, Tony picked up his pencil and tried to concentrate on the lists, but the mention of Susan Blake brought back memories of the previous year. She had been a very attractive woman. From the very beginning she had made it obvious that Tony Sheppard was just the man to amuse her during the summer. Unfortunately for Tony, he had never bothered to take her up on any of the blatant invitations she made, and when she realized that he was simply not interested in her, she became quite venomous. At times she had made things very difficult for Tony, but he had shrugged his broad shoulders and carried on with his work, indifferent to Susan's efforts. Susan had made no secret of her emotions and every member of the staff had known and understood the circumstances. So had her employer. At the end of the season Howard had told Susan not to return the following year as she was a trouble-maker and a bad influence in the camp. He had not known then that Gail was willing to take Susan's place as his secretary, but he had decided he would rather have an indifferent worker who was popular with the staff than an efficient woman who antagonized everyone and brought an alien atmosphere into the camp.

Tony wondered idly what Howard's new secretary would be like—would she play on her relationship to the camp owner? He thought it strange that Blair was determined to grant her no special favours, but, thinking it over, he realized that it was the wisest thing to do. At least no petty jealousies would be aroused. He assumed that Blair did not want the relationship to be broadcast to the rest of the staff and he thought it wise.

Howard was very popular with his staff. He had little to do with the campers, seldom mixing with them, but the staff knew him well and appreciated his kindness, his fairness and his consideration for their welfare and happiness.

Leaving the Main Building, Howard walked back to the Office Block. This housed the Reception Office—a long room with one wall made entirely of glass and with several bays for dealing with incoming campers. Murals adorned the walls: occasional tables and chairs stood around the room and a line of telephone booths occupied one corner. The Block also contained his private office, a smaller office for his secretary, a large room used for staff conferences, and one or two other rooms. A young woman sat at a typewriter in the Conference Room. It was her job to organize the table positions in the dining-hall for the campers and this involved much thought and attention to detail. The children had their own dining-hall and their meals were provided half-an-hour before their parents' eating-times. Clare Marshall was in charge of the Catering Department which dealt with the employment of kitchen staff and waitresses, the supervision of their work, the ordering of provisions, the preparation of the menus: the cafeteria also came under her jurisdiction. It was a most important position. Clare was very capable and highly efficient.

Howard had always found her assistance invaluable. She had been with the camp since the first season, six years ago, and they were good friends by this time. She was a dark-haired, attractive woman in her late twenties: she dressed smartly and neatly; she invited confidence and found popularity with both staff and campers because of her pleasant manner and ready charm.

He opened the door of the Conference Room and looked in. 'How are you getting on?' he asked.

Clare looked up from her typewriter. 'Fine,' she replied. 'The first weeks are never so bad—it's mid-season when I start to count the grey hairs!'

Howard laughed. He entered and went to look over her shoulder at the typescript. She smiled up at him. 'Why not give it a rest?' he asked. 'You've been at it all morning.'

Clare shook her head. 'I daren't leave it now,' she replied. 'I've almost finished, Howard.'

'Come and have some tea with me when you reach the end,' he invited.

'I'd love to,' she told him warmly.

He nodded, rumpled her short dark hair with an affectionate gesture, and left her to her work. She looked after his stocky figure with warmth in her brown eyes and then, with a sigh, she turned back to her typewriter.

Howard entered his own office, feeling the familiar surge of pleasure and satisfaction. It was large, spacious and comfortably furnished. Clare always told him laughingly that it was more of a sitting-room than an office. Windows overlooked the flower-gardens: men were working now on the rockeries and flower-beds with colourful plants and flowers. The Office Block was expansive, white-painted and built on a higher level than the rest of the camp. This enabled Howard to see most of the camp layout from his office window: the long blocks of neat chalets, the concrete paths which ran alongside the blocks, the green lawns around whose squareness the chalets had been erected in blocks of ten, the Main Building to the right, the swimming-pool with its high diving-boards and concrete surrounds to the left, the children's playgrounds, the path which led to the stables, and, behind the chalets, the playing-fields for cricket, football,

11

netball and other strenuous games.

Howard was very proud of the camp, which had been his own idea, built from his own plans and launched with his own money. He had been fortunate that his father had been an industrial magnate who had left the majority of his millions to his son, Howard, and only a small annuity to his daughter who had married a man that none of the family could willingly accept. This had always seemed most unfair to Howard, but he could do nothing about his father's will and Mary had always been too proud to accept any of what she called 'charity' from her brother. Hubert Anson had been a fairly successful man, so he had been able to keep his wife in the kind of luxury to which she had become accustomed!

It was a far cry from the huge mansion in which she and her brother had been born and reared, but though she found it difficult at first to cut her coat according to her cloth, she learnt the hard way! She only had one child, her daughter Gail: Howard had never married—he called the camp his child and loved it as such. He had every reason to be proud of the beautiful surroundings in which the holiday-makers spent a brief respite from their everyday life: no expense had ever been spared, yet Howard managed to keep the tariff at a reasonably low level.

Looking over the camp with the familiar feelings of pride and inner satisfaction,

Howard thought of Gail—he had always been fond of the child who reminded him so vividly of his sister Mary. It had been a shock to learn a few months previously of his sister's death, but he had written to Gail promising her any help, financial or otherwise, that she might need. Her letter in reply asked him if he could offer her a job at his holiday camp and assured him that she had taken an excellent secretarial course before leaving school—she had not put her knowledge to good use because her mother had been ill for several years before her death and Gail had run the home and nursed her mother without complaint or selfish desire to lead her own life. Her plea had come at an opportune moment, for Howard had been thinking of advertising for a secretary to take Susan Blake's place.

He felt sure that Gail would settle down easily at the camp and soon make friends with the staff. It had been her request that their relationship be kept a secret and, a little reluctantly, he had agreed. He was a man who felt pride of possession, no matter whether it was a successful holiday camp, a favourite book or painting, or merely an attractive niece, but he was shrewd enough to see the snags which might arise if it was generally known that Gail Anson was related to the owner of the camp.

CHAPTER TWO

Gail Anson hurriedly fished for a mirror in her handbag and glanced at her reflection: it had been a long journey from her home in Dorset and she knew that her small face was looking pale and tired, her blue eyes were not so bright and merry as usual, and her dark hair was rumpled and falling over her brow. But there was little time now to tidy herself: she had fallen asleep on the train and her fellow-passenger had just woken her to inform her that Combleigh was the next stop. They had exchanged a few polite, tentative remarks at the beginning of the journey.

He was a tall man and he reached up for her case with little effort as they ran into the small station which was little more than a halt. She thanked him with a smile. He nodded briefly and resumed his seat. An elderly business man (though he thought of her as a charming little thing), he had not bothered to make conversation, glad when she had drifted into sleep soon after they left the London terminus, leaving him free to concentrate on his newspaper and the crossword.

The train was a few minutes late. Gail stepped down from the compartment. Her companion of the last two hours handed her down the light case. She slammed the door shut and looked about her eagerly. It was some years since she had seen her uncle and for a brief moment she felt shy and nervous.

A slim, fair-headed man moved towards her, almost uncertainly. When he reached her, he said: 'Excuse me, I'm from Blair Holiday Camp. Are you Gail Anson, by any chance?'

She flashed a quick smile that was tinged with relief. 'Yes, that's right,' she replied.

'I'm Johnny Greer,' he told her. 'The car's waiting outside the station.' He took her case from her and she went through the station barrier, handing in her ticket. He nodded to the ticket collector who knew him well. Few passengers had alighted from the train, but in the height of the season hordes of campers would invade Combleigh's small station each Saturday.

A new Ford saloon car stood in the forecourt and Johnny moved towards it, followed by Gail. He threw her case into the back of the car and opened the door for his passenger. Then, moving around to the other side, he slipped into the driving seat and turned on the ignition.

'How far is the camp?' Gail asked eagerly.

'Just over a mile,' he replied. 'We meet the trains with special coaches for the campers.' He pulled out of the forecourt into the small High Street with its medley of shops.

'What do you do?'

'Me? I'm the Assistant Organizer,' Johnny

15

said, with a smile. 'General dog's-body, actually, but it's great fun.'

'I've never seen a holiday camp,' she confessed. 'I suppose there's plenty to do.'

'There's a lot of hard work when you're staff,' he told her, 'but it's worth it when the campers have a good time. Believe me, they do at Blair!' He threw her a quick glance. 'By the way, forgive me for mentioning it, but I know that you're related to Howard Blair. He told me before I came to pick you up—but I won't mention it to anyone else.'

'Was my uncle too busy to meet me himself?' she asked.

'It's a busy time for everyone with the season opening in a few weeks,' he replied. He grinned at her. 'I hate this waiting period,' he added lightly. He drove well and capably, the car gliding smoothly along the road. As they went along country lanes towards the coast, leaving the village behind, he told her something about her new surroundings.

She listened carefully, studying his good-looking profile. For Johnny was certainly good-looking: it could be a drawback when impressionable young girls on holiday developed a crush for the young Assistant Organizer with his ready smile and pleasant manner.

They drove into the camp grounds and Gail caught her breath. Johnny smiled at her proudly. 'Nice, eh?'

'Nice! They're beautiful!' She spoke of the flowerbeds, the neat gravel paths, the low white buildings. 'Everything's lovely!' she exclaimed. 'I had no idea it would be like this.'

'What did you expect?' he asked curiously. 'Wooden huts and a bit of grass?'

She laughed lightly. 'Not exactly,' she replied, 'but something on those lines.'

Gail followed Johnny up the wide steps to the Reception Office. He led her through the large, well-lit room with the decorative murals, along a corridor, paused by a door and opened it after knocking lightly.

Howard turned from the window and his eyes were very warm as he ran his gaze over Gail's pretty face. She smiled a little hesitantly. 'Gail, my dear!' he exclaimed. 'How very nice to see you!' He went over to her and kissed her cheek. Then he turned to Johnny. 'Thanks for bringing Gail from the station,' he said with a smile. 'I'm sure you're very busy—it must have been annoying to break off to drive to the station.'

Johnny shook his head. 'Not at all. Now that I've delivered the goods safely, I'll be going.' He smiled at Gail. 'See you around!' He nodded to Howard and went.

'Well, Gail—what do you think of the camp—what you've seen so far, that is?'

'It's wonderful!' she enthused. 'I think it's really lovely—the surroundings alone are worth the journey.'

17

Howard was well pleased by her reply. He moved to the telephone which stood on a low table, picked up the receiver. When the operator on the camp's private exchange replied, he asked for tea to be sent over to his office for three people.

Gail raised her eyebrows. She had loosened her pale-blue suit coat and stood by the long window, surveying the camp. But now she turned as he replaced the receiver.

'Clare Marshall will be with us in a minute,' he explained. 'She's my Catering Director and a charming person. I know you'll like her, Gail.' Even as he spoke, the door opened and Clare entered, a sheaf of papers in her hand.

As Howard introduced the two women, Gail studied the Catering Director: dark, attractive, poised. She had a lovely smile which revealed even white teeth and touched her eyes with quick warmth. On her left hand sparkled a wide golden wedding band. For her part, Clare smiled at a girl some five or six years her junior—a girl with short, black curls, blue eyes that looked as if they could smile easily, a piquant, lovely face that now was pale and tired.

The tea arrived very quickly and Clare presided over the pouring of the amber liquid. Gail gratefully accepted a hot cup of tea. She sat in one of the armchairs, slim legs crossed, her head resting on the back of the chair with obvious gratitude; Howard offered his cigarette case but she refused with a slight shake of her head. Clare took a cigarette from him with a nod of thanks.

Briefly, Howard gave his niece a résumé of camp life, the kind of duties she would be undertaking, and told her something about the planned summer season.

'Am I living at the bungalow with you?' Gail asked.

Clare also knew of the relationship, for Howard told her most things and, sensing the friendship which existed between the two people, Gail did not mind that her uncle had confided in his Catering Director. Briefly, she wondered how many people did indeed know the truth.

'No. I decided against it,' Howard said in reply to her question. 'You'll be sleeping and living in the staff quarters, Gail. As far as anyone is concerned, you're my secretary. My two Organizers know, of course, and so does Clare—but I've told no one else. I expect you'll be sharing a chalet with one of the girls, but they're a nice crowd, on the whole, and the chalets are quite luxurious. I don't think you'll suffer in any way by not living with me at the bungalow.'

Gail nodded. 'I don't mind,' she assured him. 'I'm looking forward to working here— and I don't want any favours, Uncle Howard. I'm your secretary, a member of the staff—I should feel the same way if I were your daughter and not your niece!'

'Good!' Howard approved. He smiled at her. 'Then you'd better lose the habit of calling me uncle!'

'Oh, yes!' exclaimed Gail with a light laugh. 'What shall I call you?'

'Well, there isn't any formality here. All the staff are known by their Christian names. So you must call me Blair, as many of them do, or simply Howard.'

She wrinkled her small nose. 'I can't call you Blair!' she objected. 'That seems like an insult.'

'Make it Howard then.' He turned to Clare. 'I wonder if you'd have time to take Gail along to Tony and find out the number of her chalet? I'd be grateful if you would look after her for a day or two until she settles in. Everything will be so strange to her at first.'

'Of course I will,' Clare assured him. She rose to her feet. 'Are you ready, Gail—I expect you'd like to freshen up a little.'

Gail nodded. 'I'd love a bath,' she said with a sigh.

'That's easily arranged,' Clare assured her. 'I expect you've been travelling for hours! Did you have a case with you—or were your things sent on?'

'My trunk came on last week. But I had a small case. Mr. Greer left it in the Reception Hall.'

'Johnny . . .' corrected Howard with a smile.

'He's a grand chap, Gail.'

She shrugged slightly. 'Too good-looking,' she said casually. Clare and Howard exchanged amused glances. 'He seems nice enough, though,' Gail continued, 'but it's too early to form an opinion.'

'Well, if you two don't want a few minutes' chat by yourselves, Howard, I'll carry Gail off now,' Clare said easily.

Howard put an arm about Gail's shoulders. 'We can talk later,' he said. 'Run along now and see something of the camp.'

Gail and Clare left the room and Howard stood at the window, watching the two women as they walked along the path to the Main Building. Gail had grown up since he last saw her: what was she now? he wondered—twenty-one, twenty-two! She was certainly a lovely girl —of course, she was tired now and paler than usual. She seemed very sure of herself. He smiled again at the memory of her comment on Johnny. She'd probably had her share of male admiration by this time—and was a little scornful of men. He remembered that Mary had been just the same at that age—then she had met Hubert Anson. A faint glimmer of a scowl touched Howard's features . . .

Gail looked about her with eager eyes. 'This is a lovely place,' she declared as they reached the Main Building. 'It must have cost thousands to build.'

Clare shrugged. 'In Howard's eyes, it was

21

worth every penny—because it was what he wanted to do and because the campers really enjoy themselves here!'

Gail smiled at her. 'I think I'd like to spend a holiday here,' she said with a lightness in her voice.

'It's better to work here through the summer,' Clare assured her. 'When one comes for a holiday, there's always the thought that one has to go home again so soon. Believe me, Gail, the weeks fly by, and we all dread the end of the season!'

'What do you do in the winter?'

Clare shrugged again. 'Whatever I can. Office work—exhibition demonstrator—I was a children's nurse last winter! To people like us, the winter is only a waiting period for the season and it doesn't matter very much what we do as long as we earn enough to live.'

Gail nodded. She had noticed the wedding ring and now she asked with a gleam of curiosity in her eyes: 'Does your husband work at the camp too?'

'I'm a widow,' Clare replied evenly. She had lost the husband she adored only a few months after marrying him—it was seven years ago now and she could think of him without pain. But she always wore the wedding ring he had given her.

They entered the Main Building and Clare turned towards the ballroom dais. Gail looked about her with admiration in her eyes for the gay murals on the walls, the glass-paned wall running the length of the ballroom, the general, attractive layout.

A man lounging against a door heard their footsteps and called: 'Tony isn't in his office— if that's who you're looking for!'

Clare stopped short. 'Any idea where he is?' she called across.

The man she addressed shrugged his shoulders indifferently. 'Sorry! He left his office about half-an-hour ago. He could be anywhere.'

'What a nuisance!' exclaimed Clare to Gail, but her smile was rich. 'I expect you're longing to be on your own in your own little chalet.' She sighed. 'We'll just have to scout around for Tony, that's all.'

They did not have to look very far.

It was a warm afternoon and as they left the Main Building, Clare turned as a voice hailed her. Tony had just hauled himself up out of the swimming-pool and he stood, sleeking back his wet hair, water pouring from his lithe body, grinning broadly. He had a powerful physique: broad shoulders, narrow waist and flanks. His quick breathing emphasized the big chest, the flexing of the muscles in his stomach.

Tony looked past Clare at Gail and his whole body suddenly tensed. Their eyes met and hers filled with stunned astonishment mingling with swift pleasure which faded as he stared at her, unsmiling, obviously unwilling to recognize her. She flushed a little.

'You're supposed to be working!' Clare accused, walking towards him.

'All work and no play...' He shook his head.

'This is Gail Anson, Blair's new secretary,' Clare introduced her to him. He nodded slightly.

'Hallo there!' he said casually, as though she were a stranger.

Gail quickly followed his lead, although a trace of bewilderment lurked in her blue eyes. 'Hallo,' she replied smoothly. 'That water looks inviting—I could do with a refreshing dip!'

'We've just been looking for you,' Clare informed Tony. 'I want to know Gail's chalet number—the poor girl is worn out from travelling.'

'Oh Lord, I can't remember!' he retorted. 'Just a minute.' He grabbed a thick towel from a wooden seat. He rubbed his wet body and his dark hair. Then he slipped his feet into sandals and pulled on a yellow sweater. 'Let's go and find out,' he said. He led the way back to the Main Building. It was an easy matter to check the staff lists and he soon found the chalet number he had allotted to Gail. 'You'll be sharing it with Ann Mathers, but she won't be here for another two weeks or so,' he told her, hardly glancing at her. 'You'll be able to live in solitary luxury for a while.'

She wondered if he really did not remember her or if his lack of recognition was deliberate.

He suggested buying them each a cold drink before Clare took Gail to her chalet and they sat at a table in the cafeteria which was partly open for the use of the staff who had come early to the camp. Tony seemed unconcerned that he still wore his wet swimming shorts and that a pool was slowly forming beneath his chair from the water that dripped from his still-wet body. They sipped ice cream sodas through straws while Clare and Tony kept up a rapid, gay conversation. They told Gail a lot about the camp but Tony addressed her with an easy casualness which did not hint at their former friendship and Clare had no idea that they had known each other before this meeting.

Many stopped to speak to Tony and Clare: others called across the room or waved in passing; everyone was smiling, happy and friendly.

Gail was content to listen while they talked with animation about the camp, the holiday-makers, the staff, their living quarters and all the facilities of the camp which the staff enjoyed. It seemed that Tony made a point of enjoying himself as much as possible at the camp: he obviously believed in working hard and playing hard.

At last he rose. 'I won't keep you from your chalet any longer,' he told Gail with an easy yet guarded smile. 'Besides, I've work to do.'

Gail watched him walk across the ballroom to his office with a lithe grace. Later, in the quiet peace of her chalet, she thought of Tony Sheppard and wondered why he so obviously wanted to forget that they had ever been friends in the past. She wondered if she would have a chance to speak to him alone—to find out if his casualness was deliberate or if he had not recognized her. The latter just didn't seem possible when she recalled how close they had been at one time . . .

CHAPTER THREE

That evening, Howard gave a small dinner-party at the bungalow: occasionally throughout the season he invited members of his staff to dine with him and one and all looked forward to such evenings: he invited Clare, Tony and Johnny on this occasion. It was an intimate, private gathering to welcome Gail to the camp—both as his niece and his secretary.

Tony arrived in a dark-blue suit which was exquisitely tailored and immaculate: Johnny chose a pale-green light tweed suit which emphasized his fair colouring. Gail studied both men as they entered, finding it difficult to decide which of them was the most handsome. They were both blessed with striking good looks—Tony as dark as Johnny was fair. But, perhaps because of his fairness, Johnny seemed very boyish and youthful against the dark, mature magnetism of his colleague—the same magnetism which had first attracted Gail to Tony Sheppard three years previously.

She was wearing pink: a pretty dress with a full skirt and a low neckline. The colour emphasized her dark hair and reflected in her cheeks. Clare wore a gown of soft wine material: a sombre, sophisticated dress which emphasized her maturity as against Gail's soft youth.

The meal was excellent: conversation was light, rapid and humorous; after they had eaten, coffee was served in the lounge. The bungalow was low, long and furnished throughout in a contemporary style. Its expensive *décor* reflected the tastes of its owner and designer, Howard Blair.

Johnny came to sit beside Gail on a comfortable studio couch. 'I can't understand why you're going to live in the staff quarters,' he said easily. 'There's plenty of room in this place for you and your uncle.'

Gail shrugged her slim shoulders. 'I expect my uncle has his reasons,' she said lightly. 'As for me, I'm happy with the chalet. It's very nice and there's plenty of room for two people.'

'Will you like living with a strange girl?' he asked.

'Why not? I've been to boarding school—and one shares dormitories with other girls there. It won't worry me.' She laid a hand briefly on his arm. 'Tell me—do you know my room-mate, Ann Mathers? What is she like?'

'Ann? She's a very nice girl.' His eyes lit with enthusiasm. 'Friendly and jolly—so you're sharing with Ann? I'm pleased about it because I think you'll like her, Gail.'

During dinner they had sat together and formality had soon been banished. Gail had formed a liking for the young man earlier, despite her careless, almost contemptuous remark to Howard about Johnny Greer. She found him very easy to talk to, amusing, companionable, with an infectious smile and twinkling, bright blue eyes.

'I hope so,' she replied now. She laughed softly, lightly. 'I'm sure there must be a snag somewhere, Johnny. Everyone I've met so far has been nice—it just can't be possible that all Blair staff are blessed with similar qualities!'

Tony overheard this remark and he called across the room: 'Oh, we've all got horns and a tail, really.'

She looked up quickly and met his eyes. He was talking to Clare and now he leaned back, perfectly at his ease, cigarette dangling from long fingers, a smile playing about his lips. He was certainly handsome. She felt a trace of the old fascination for him steal through her veins. Tony's eyes looked deep into hers. Her heart skipped a beat and, disconcerted, she rose and placed her cup on a low coffee table. Howard caught her arm and drew her towards him, engaging her in conversation. But while she talked to her uncle, gay and animated, she was certain that Tony still gazed at her and her blood was confused.

She turned slightly to glance at him from beneath long lashes. She knew a surge of disappointment for he was certainly not watching her. He bent over Clare, giving her a light for her cigarette. Had she imagined that his gaze scorched her back, Gail wondered?

Later, she wandered through the big, open

29

windows on to the terrace which overlooked flower-gardens and in the distance the white buildings of the camp. The bungalow was about eighty yards from the camp grounds, secluded and private.

Tony followed her out of the lounge. He stood for a moment at the door and she was unconscious of his presence. Then he moved towards her, taking a cigarette from a packet he took from his pocket. He thrust it between his lips and flicked a lighter into flame. She turned quickly to look up into his illumined face. A question sparked in her lovely eyes. He waited until his cigarette was property alight and the lighter replaced in his pocket. Then he said drily: 'It's a small world.'

'I thought you'd forgotten me,' she said quickly.

He raised one eyebrow in a quizzical gesture. 'Surely you would be the first to think that impossible?'

She flushed slightly at his mocking words. 'I recognized you,' she pointed out.

'I haven't changed,' he retorted. 'After all, it's only three years.' He glanced at her sharply. 'I was rather surprised when Blair spoke of you as his niece.'

'There wasn't time for you to know much about me,' she replied in a low voice.

He smiled. 'You did leave Stella's place rather abruptly,' he reminded her. 'I often wondered if I was to blame for that.'

They had met at a friend's home. Gail had been persuaded by her invalid mother to spend a holiday with an old school-friend and reluctantly she had agreed on the proviso that her father hired a private nurse for the time she would be away. Tony Sheppard had also been staying with the Cleggs, for he was a friend of the two sons of the family. It was early in the year before the summer season at Blair Holiday Camp called him. He had started a mild flirtation with the pretty Gail Anson which had developed with startling suddenness into something warmer. Only eighteen at the time and having led a sheltered, lonely life since leaving school, Gail had been swept off her feet by the good looks and charm of Tony Sheppard. Amused but not deeply affected, Tony had made it very clear that with their departure from the Cleggs' house the affair ended. Hurt and bewildered, Gail had cut her visit short and they had not met since—until today when she arrived at Blair Holiday Camp to become her uncle's secretary.

'My mother was ill,' she retorted sharply. She had long since mocked and chided herself for succumbing to this man's charms and she had no intention of knowing again the same humiliation that she had suffered. It had been painful to realize that the affair had meant nothing to him, while she had readily given her youthful heart. But she had time enough to realize that her mother needed her too much for her to think of marriage or love affairs and she admitted to herself that her hurt emotions had soon healed.

'Yes, I remember that was the excuse,' he said with a faint smile. 'I hope she soon recovered.'

'My mother died three months ago,' she said curtly.

Instantly he regretted his remark. 'I'm sorry,' he said gently. 'She was ill a long time?'

'Several years.'

He brought out his cigarettes. 'Will you have one of these?' he asked, offering the packet. 'You never used to smoke, but I expect you've learnt the habit.'

She shook her head. 'No, thank you—I've tried it once or twice but I don't enjoy it.'

He put them away again. 'Well, what do you think of Blair so far?'

'I think I shall like it here,' she said slowly. 'It was rather a shock to find that you were the Chief Organizer here, Tony. I can't associate you with this kind of career.'

'Why not?' His tone was slightly defensive. 'I've been with Blair since the camp opened. It's a grand job and I love it. Howard's fine to work for—we get on very well together.'

Gail nodded. 'I'm looking forward to the start of the season,' she said. 'I imagine it must all seem so much more worth while when the place is swarming with holiday-makers.'

'Yes,' he agreed. 'It's very noisy and human and enjoyable.'

'Do you mean to continue to act as though I were a perfect stranger?' she asked abruptly.

He shrugged. 'It's rather difficult to admit to a previous acquaintance now,' he said. 'But friendships spring up quickly here—no two people are strangers after a day or so.'

There was a brief pause. Gail looked up into his face and an enigmatic smile touched her lips. 'Then I can bank on your friendship, Tony?'

He dropped his cigarette to the paved floor of the terrace and ground his heel on it. Then he said lightly: 'You'll find that friendships formed at a holiday camp are warm and impetuous but superficial and short-lived.' He looked across at the white buildings of the camp. 'So many ships that pass in the night, Gail—I think that every year—every week—every day. I watch the campers eagerly seeking new friendships, new excitements—a boy and a girl meet here on the first day of their holiday: they are together all day and every day, reluctant to part even for the few short hours of the night: they exchange addresses and photographs and vows of lasting affection when it comes to the end of their holiday— then they return to their familiar, normal way of life and within a few days have forgotten each other. The adults follow the same pattern—determined to keep up a friendship

33

formed here, convinced that their new friends have everything in common with them—as soon as they get back to the old routine all their good intentions of writing and meeting fade away. If they do meet again—just once—they come away wondering what they saw in each other in the first place.' His voice took on a cynical note.

'Surely it isn't always like that?' Gail said slowly.

'In nine cases out of ten,' he retorted. 'Of course, some of our young couples do marry and come back here for their honeymoon—but it's rare enough for Howard to present them with a cheque for fifty pounds as a wedding present when that happens!'

'Isn't it the same in ordinary social circles?' Gail countered. 'One is for ever meeting new people and taking them at face value—considering them to be charming and kind and sincere. But so often they are nothing of the sort!'

Tony looked down at her. 'I think it depends on how one reacts to meeting new people. You're naturally impulsive and sociable. You enjoy making new friends and eagerly offer your own friendship, don't you? I take my time about people—I like to sum them up carefully and reserve my judgment until I'm really sure. Then, if they prove themselves worthy of it, I give them my friendship.'

'If you're going to analyse every person you meet, I imagine you'll make very few friends in life,' she told him sharply.

He laughed. 'I have friends enough now,' he said easily. 'I've no wish to add to the list.'

A swift flush surged to stain her cheeks. 'I see that I was wrong in thinking we could be friends, Tony.' She brushed past him. 'Excuse me, will you? It's getting a little chilly out here.'

Tony looked after her with a faint smile quirking his lips. Gail had quickly taken offence at his words, but he had not meant to be offensive. It was a strange coincidence that she should turn out to be Howard Blair's niece. He sent his memory back to the time three years ago when they had met at the Cleggs' home. She had been pretty, sweet and affectionate then. Warm-hearted and impulsive—a little too eagerly impulsive, Tony reminded himself, remembering her reaction to his light-hearted attentions; it was his nature to flirt with every pretty woman with no more in mind than a pleasing pastime which both enjoyed. But Gail Anson had reacted far more violently than he had expected and his smile now was for the youthful, naïve innocence she had shown, the simple candour, the impulsive giving of her affections—like all the young, it had not occurred to her that they might be rebuffed. A little shaken, more than a little sympathetic, Tony had decided to be cruel in order to be kind to the girl. He had made it obvious that she meant nothing more than a light flirtation. If he had encouraged her further, she would have known far more pain later, for Tony was a lone wolf with no intention of marriage. He had never met a woman who could stir him deeply: he doubted if he ever would; he was an independent man who liked his freedom and he could not visualize sacrificing it on the altar of love.

Gail entered the lounge, hoping that her hot cheeks had cooled. She joined Clare and Johnny and entered their conversation, striving for composure, though hurt pride and annoyance fought within her for prior place. How dare he! It was the second time he had told her bluntly that he was not interested in her: she would not give him the opportunity to chalk up a third. She could manage without his friendship!

While she talked and smiled, ignoring Tony's entry a few minutes later, her thoughts continued to tease her anger. Speaking of disappointment, she had certainly been deceived by Tony Sheppard. First acquaintance had led her to think him personable, friendly, likeable and charming— she had once liked him too much, but she had long since recovered from that. But through the years she had carried a warm memory of him and a hope that they would meet again. Now she felt positive dislike for the man, remembering his blatant rudeness, his obvious lack of interest in her, and his detestable cynicism.

She had often shrunk from the memory of her behaviour three years ago—her eagerness to shower affection on Tony, her embarrassing insistence to share all his waking moments, the way she had spoken openly of the warm emotion she felt for him, the revelation of the dreams which she had fostered in her youthful heart. Afterwards, she had forgiven Tony and sympathized with him for the position in which she had placed him and the action she had forced him to take.

Now it seemed that Tony remembered vividly too and feared a second such performance on her part: she cursed her impulsiveness which had led her to speak warmly to him, asking for his friendship. But she would not repeat her mistake. In future, she would be coolly polite to him and surely their paths would not cross too often—she was employed in the office and he was here, there and everywhere as the organizer. Tony Sheppard would have no further cause to think that she was 'chasing' him—but the phrase again caused her cheeks to glow . . .

CHAPTER FOUR

Gail threw herself into the spirit of the camp and found that she enjoyed not only the office work which kept her occupied all day but also the atmosphere, the friendly chaffing of the other staff, the kind helpfulness of Clare Marshall, and the facilities for enjoyment which the camp offered. She quickly made friends with those of the staff who were already at the camp and they accepted her as one of themselves without question.

On Thursday morning, Gail turned up at the office and uncovered her typewriter, drawing folders toward her, and preparing for work.

Howard came into the room some minutes later. He was surprised to see Gail seated at her desk, her nimble fingers tapping the keys.

'Gail, what are you doing here?' he asked. She glanced up at him with a puzzled smile.

'Working, of course,' she replied lightly.

'I can see that,' he retorted. 'But didn't Tony tell you that Thursday is your day off?'

She shook her head. 'He certainly didn't.' She had barely exchanged more than a few words with Tony since the night of the dinner-party at the bungalow. It was not difficult to avoid him, for they both had their individual work to do during the day, and in the evenings

38

Gail played tennis with her new-found friends or explored the camp grounds or walked along the beach in the direction of the village.

'Well, it is,' Howard assured her firmly. 'All day on Thursday and from lunchtime on Sunday. It doesn't seem a lot, I know, but it won't always be so much like hard work, my dear. When the season is well under way, you'll find lots of time to enjoy yourself in the week, apart from your time off.'

Gail began to re-cover her machine. 'I've a lot of work to do now,' she said. 'Are you sure you want me to have today off? After all, I've only been here three days—I don't mind giving it up.'

'Nonsense!' Howard exclaimed. He put a hand on her shoulder. 'You're a good girl, Gail, and a good worker. I'm already thankful that you wanted to come and work for me.'

She smiled up at him. 'So am I! I love it here.'

'I thought you might! It's a good life—old or young. Talk to any of the staff and you'll find that they'd never give up holiday-camp work. Fortunately for me, they like Blairs, too.'

'I'm not surprised!' she told him with some heat. 'This is a wonderful camp—and you're a good boss. The work may be hard—but there's time to play, too!'

Howard smiled. 'It is hard work,' he said slowly. 'You've proved that already. But the season hasn't started yet. We'll have a few complaints from the staff then, my dear—and you'll hear all about those!'

'What sort of complaints?'

Howard shrugged. 'Not enough time off, for one thing. Too little time to get the tables laid up and all ready for each meal. Complaints about the chalets, about the hot water system, about the campers—' He grinned. 'You'll find out, Gail.'

'If anyone could complain, then they must be very ungrateful,' Gail said quickly. '*I* think everything is wonderful.'

'Ah—but human beings are ungrateful wretches for the most part,' Howard told her lightly. 'The more you do for some people—the more they want you to do for them! The only ones who don't complain, as a rule, are those who pay for the privilege of living at Blairs for a week or two—the campers!' He chuckled. 'We get the occasional hard-to-please customer, of course—but when the complaints become wholesale, then I shall know it's time to close the camp for good.'

Gail rose from her desk and gathered up the folders, tidying them, putting them into neat bundles.

'Leave those, Gail,' Howard said quickly. 'I came in to look up some figures—I shall want them during the day.' Gail nodded and turned towards the door. 'You can take the camp car if you like and go into Midleigh,' he said, absently, searching through one of the files.

Midleigh was the nearest big town and shopping centre and Gail had been hoping for the opportunity to explore it.

'I can't drive,' she said ruefully. 'I don't hold a licence, either.'

'We'll have to get Johnny to teach you,' Howard said lightly. 'You'll find it a useful asset here. The buses are pretty infrequent until the season starts, then the local company runs two an hour. Quite a lot of people slip into Midleigh for an hour or so, to look round the shops.'

Gail nodded. 'I could use a new swimsuit,' she said. 'I thought mine would be all right—until I saw Clare in the pool yesterday. I liked her costume very much.'

Howard smiled. 'Clare's dress sense is perfect,' he said approvingly. 'She'd make a good adviser if you decide to buy any clothes while you're here.'

'I'll remember that!' Gail promised lightly, then she bade him a cheery farewell. She left the big Office Block, humming to herself happily. Turning a corner, she almost collided with Johnny.

'Hallo ! Not working today?' he asked, with a steadying hand on her arm.

'I've just been told that it's my day off,' she said. 'I wish Tony had mentioned it—I could have enjoyed an extra hour in bed this morning.'

'It's my day off, too,' he said with real

41

pleasure. 'I always have Thursday because it's one day when there isn't much doing—apart from rehearsals for the Camper's Concert, and Tony supervises those. He produces the Concert, you know.' He grinned. 'I have to be back by six, of course, as I'm always in the Concert.'

'What do you do, Johnny?' Gail asked quickly with interest lighting her eyes and voice.

He shrugged. 'I don't possess much entertainment value—except making a fool of myself! I'm expert at that!'

Gail laughed. They stood talking for a few more minutes, then Johnny said: 'Would you like to come into Midleigh with me, Gail? It's not much of a town, but it's better than Combleigh. I'll ask Howard if I can have the camp car.'

'He's already told me that I can,' she said, 'only I can't drive. I'd love to go with you, Johnny.'

'How long will you be?' he asked.

'Give me half an hour, will you? I want to change.'

He nodded. 'O.K. I'll have the car in front of Reception in half an hour.'

They parted and Gail hurried to her chalet.

It was brick-built, pleasant, the walls distempered a soft shade of yellow: bright yellow curtains hung at the long window and yellow bedspreads covered the twin beds; a

42

table stood between the two beds with a lamp on it. Gail had brought a small portable radio with her and this also stood on the table. There was a big wardrobe with sliding doors: it contained plenty of space and Gail had been careful to hang her dresses in only one half of the wardrobe, leaving room for her chalet-mate when she arrived. A long, narrow mirror had been fastened to one wall of the chalet and there was a gleaming white enamel wash-basin with hot and cold water taps, a white cabinet to one side and a shelf for soaps and other such toilet articles. There were two small chests of drawers, one at each side of the beds.

Gail considered the chalet to be very comfortable. It was very spacious for one person, and as she changed she wondered briefly if her chalet-mate's arrival would make a great deal of difference. Possibly they would be falling over each other some of the time—early morning, for instance, when they were both sleepy and yet conscious of the demanding day ahead of them.

The chalet contained all the necessities one could possibly want. It was identical to the chalets used by the campers during their brief stay—and Gail reminded herself that they had to pay for the luxury of their surroundings.

Johnny was waiting for her in the car and she hurried to join him. She had changed from her severe black suit into a pretty summer cotton dress and Johnny's glance was approving. Because she was a member of the office staff, Gail did not come under the ruling of yellow and grey outfits. She was thankful for this, sure that it would eventually become monotonous to wear the same outfits week after week, without change. She could wear whatever she liked and she thought a suit or a plain dress was most suitable for the office; but in her own time she would wear her prettiest clothes. She had not been at the camp long enough yet to realize that informality was always the order of the day.

Johnny wore his grey slacks and yellow sweater still and she teased him about this. 'Surely you'd be glad to wear your own clothes on your time off?' she asked him as they drove along the coast road towards Midleigh. The tide was high and the sea was very blue, reflecting the azure colour of the cloudless sky. 'Don't you get bored with the everlasting yellow and grey?'

He looked at her in surprise. 'If I changed into other clothes,' he said, 'no one would know that I came from Blair.'

'Do you want them to know?'

'Yes, of course. I'm proud of the camp, proud of my job—and I like it when people in the town turn round to tell their friends that I'm one of the Blair staff.' He grinned. 'The campers like to see the familiar colours, too, if they're exploring Midleigh. Besides, I like yellow, and these sweaters are very comfortable.'

'Tell me about Midleigh.' Gail gave up.

'It's only a small town. The shops aren't bad, though. There are a couple of cinemas and a small theatre. Sometimes I slip in to see a film, but I prefer to spend my free time in a quiet way: change from noise and having to entertain others, and being in a crowd.'

'But you love it all, don't you?' she asked him.

'Of course I do.' He showed even, white teeth in a broad smile. 'I couldn't do the job if I didn't love it. I can't afford to wake up in the morning and think: "Oh Lord! that crowd again!"' Gail laughed at his grimace. 'We get some fine crowds here at Blair. I love 'em all! I hate taking my free time—only Tony insists on it.' He glanced at Gail. 'Not that he bothers to take his, most of the time.'

'I'm glad I came to work at the camp,' Gail said suddenly, sincerely. She surprised herself by the eager vehemence of her tone. 'I know I'm going to enjoy every minute of it. I wish the season would hurry up and start.'

He smiled in sympathy with her feelings and impatience. 'It all seems such a waste, doesn't it?' he asked quietly. 'Everything ready and waiting for the campers—and only a handful of us in the camp to enjoy this glorious weather, to frolic in the pool and romp on the beach.' He shook his head. 'Still, not long now—and we'll be cursing the campers and their noisy little brats under our breath!' There was a warmth in his tone which took the sting from the words.

'Do you get many children?' Gail wanted to know.

'Lord, yes! Hundreds,' he said. There was a faint trace of exaggeration. 'Camps like Blair are a godsend to people with young children,' he explained. 'No trouble at all to them— parents can almost forget that they have children! With girls looking after them all day, girls supervising the mealtimes, attending to the young babies—nappy-changing, bottle-feeding and what-have-you—baby patrol at night so that anxious parents know immediately when their infants need attention . . . it's a godsend,' he repeated. 'A welcome break for both parents and children.'

'But you get young people as well as family parties, surely?'

'Of course.' Johnny grinned. 'Blair's rather noted as a romantic camp. Quite a few weddings come about from holiday meetings here—and we sometimes get the couples back on honeymoon. We've only been going six years so we haven't had much time to get them back with their children, as well—but it's happened once or twice.'

Gail laughed. 'Must be the sea air,' she teased lightly, but she thought in passing of Tony's words on the same subject and approved the lack of cynicism in Johnny's voice.

'Something like that!' he agreed as they turned into a busy shopping centre. 'Well, here we are!' he announced. 'The Metropolis of Midleigh. I'll find a decent place to park the car then we'll have a look round the shops. Or would you like coffee first?'

'Coffee first,' Gail decided, glancing at the neat little watch she wore on her wrist. 'I'm parched!'

Johnny nodded and devoted his attention to finding a suitable parking spot along the High Street.

Gail looked about her. It was a busy and friendly little town: the shop windows were well-dressed and colourful; the High Street was milling with shoppers, but Johnny assured her that in the season it did a far brisker trade, catering for their own visitors as well as those who came in from the camp.

After coffee, they strolled along the High Street. Johnny was very patient with Gail's eager window-shopping, the constant pauses, her bright chatter. He waited for her while she stopped at a big store to buy a swimsuit and a pair of sandals. She quickly made her purchases and hurried out to join her companion. For a moment, he was out of sight and she stopped short, a slight frown creasing her brow. Then he moved back into view and she hurried across to him.

'I thought I'd lost you,' she told him lightly.

He smiled down at her bright, pretty face. 'Do you want to do any more shopping?' She shook her head.

'Then let's cut through this side street on to the promenade,' he suggested, taking her arm lightly. 'It's an attractive place—Midleigh. It has a bay, you know, and the usual golden sands for this part of the coast. If you like walking, we could go right along to the end of the promenade and walk to the top of the cliffs. It's quiet and peaceful and very lovely—my favourite spot, in fact.'

Gail assented readily and they set off. She found Johnny Greer a pleasant companion and was perfectly content with him. As he had told her, it was an attractive coastline with the bay and cliffs on either side cutting the beach off from the rest of the coast. The tide was in, lapping gently against the sea wall and the high breakwaters which ran down the beach. A small pier ran out into the water and held the usual conglomeration of amusement stalls and booths.

Although it was early May, it was nevertheless very warm weather and a few people were taking advantage of the sun, reclining in deck-chairs along the top of the sea wall. Children were clambering up and down the supports of the pier and racing along the promenade or playing happily at the edge of the water. Here and there, old salts had hauled their boats up from the beach and were scaling the bottoms or overhauling the sides, getting ready for the influx of summer visitors who would queue up for the pleasure of a trip round the bay or out to the distant lighthouse.

The row of cafés and ice-cream booths and photographic studio cabins were newly-painted, bright in the sunshine, and in the background the private houses which served as hotels during the season looked as though they had recently been spring-cleaned, inside and out, their windows gleaming, curtains newly-washed and fluttering in a warm breeze, new paint glistening and gardens neatly tended and tidied.

Gail loved walking and she strode along beside Johnny, chattering away to him, asking him eager questions. While he listened and answered, he was forming his opinion of the girl by his side. That he liked her, he had known from the start: now he learnt that she was bright and eager, obviously intelligent, amusing, a girl of impulsive warmth and natural candour, friendly, sociable and certainly very likeable; he glanced down at her pretty face, noting the shining eyes with the long, thick lashes, the small, straight nose, the full, generous mouth and the pointed, determined chin which lent a hint of piquancy to her small face. He approved the short, dark hair cut in a fashionable urchin style, the casual cotton dress, the low-heeled sandals, the easy grace of her movements and her obvious enjoyment of life. That she was very young he knew, but the mature, sophisticated woman awed him: he liked and admired Clare Marshall, for instance, but he was never completely at his ease when in her company. He felt drawn to Gail because she was so young and amusing and eager to please—she asked his opinion and waited eagerly for the answer—she smiled up at him with a friendly light and something like admiration in her deep blue eyes—as they climbed the steep road to the top of the cliff, her fingers sought his naturally for assistance and she laughed easily at his mock display of exhaustion as they neared the top. He did not analyse his reaction as pleasure at simple flattery: he merely decided that Gail Anson was sweet and charming and fun to be with and therefore an asset to the camp.

They reached the top and sank down on the thick grass of the cliff. In the distance could be seen the gleaming, golden beach which was part of Blair Holiday Camp and the trees which surrounded the white buildings to ensure its privacy from the road which ran past the camp to Midleigh from Combleigh. The sea below glistened in the sunlight, calm and beautiful. The cliff-top had been cultivated by the local council and bright, colourful flower-beds separated by white concrete paths made the Cliff Walk attractive and popular. A bandstand had been erected and a brass band played there in the afternoons during the season, surrounded by deck-chairs on a white concrete surround.

Where Johnny and Gail sat green grass grew wild—they had left the council path and made their own way across the green, sweet-scented cliff-top, heads held high as they breathed deeply of the healthy ozone and lifted their faces to the breeze which was stronger yet still warm.

Later, they lunched in Midleigh and then went to one of the cinemas, where they sat in the darkness and laughed together at a musical comedy film. They held hands and exchanged amused glances, whispered conspiratorially together and knew a great contentment in each other's company.

As evening drew near, they reluctantly drove back to the camp, both conscious that the day had been a delightful one, and both knowing a strange intimacy, a feeling that they had been friends for years.

Gail thought of Tony's words—*'friendships spring up quickly here'*—and the truth of his remark was brought home to her as she glanced at the already-dear profile of the man by her side and her eyes held a warm, affectionate light.

CHAPTER FIVE

The days sped by at the camp. Gail was very happy, working through the day at her typewriter, constantly finding out fresh information about her new home, throwing herself into the spirit of the place with zest and energy and enthusiasm. In the evenings, she strengthened her new friendship with Johnny Greer and enjoyed the company of others on the staff who had accepted her very quickly as one of themselves. She found time too for the necessary chores—washing, ironing, sewing, writing letters.

After the first glorious days when the sun shone down benevolently and the gentle breeze was warm and pleasant, the weather changed suddenly. For nearly a week, Gail rose in the mornings to look out of her chalet window at leaden, heavy skies. Rain fell continually, with only short dry intervals. She was thankful for her thick sweaters and sensible brogues, for it was cold as well as wet. The daily newspapers told her that all of England was enduring the same depressing rain.

The staff ran from building to building in the torrential rain, raincoats held over their shoulders or protecting their heads, laughing and joking about the weather. Gail was surprised to find how lightly they took the constant cold, depressing rain.

The following Thursday Johnny came in search of Gail and found her thumbing dispiritedly through the books in the Campers' Library. He raised a quizzical eye at her dejection.

'Would you like to go into Midleigh with me?' he asked. 'Or is it too wet?'

She turned to him eagerly. 'It can't be any wetter in Midleigh than it is here, Johnny. I'd love to go—I can't find anything to do, anyway.'

He grinned. 'That's what I thought.'

Parking the car in the High Street, they ran along the wet pavements to a café. The downpour drenched them but they arrived breathless with laughter. They went in and sat down at a window table. Johnny took out his handkerchief and mopped his wet face ruefully. Not many people were about and Gail, brushing back her damp hair with her fingers, could understand their preference to stay indoors on such a day. They ordered steaming, fragrant coffee and Johnny brought out a packet of cigarettes. Gail looked out on to the wet town and the occasional hurrying shopper in mackintosh and carrying an umbrella.

Suddenly, Gail sneezed. Her expression was so startled that Johnny began to laugh. Gail's eyes twinkled across the table at him. 'Come to the sunny South Coast and catch pneumonia!' she joked.

'It isn't always like this,' he assured her. 'It's early still, Gail—and Blair has the reputation for having the most sunshine on the South Coast.'

She raised a quizzical eyebrow. 'You surprise me!' she mocked.

'It was lovely last week,' he reminded her.

She relented and smiled warmly. 'Yes, it was lovely—but I don't think we'll indulge in any cliff-climbing today, Johnny.' After a moment, she said slowly: 'It must be very disappointing for the campers when it rains. They wait all year for a week's holiday at Blair and if they get a week like this one—well!'

Johnny nodded. 'But we don't get many grumbles,' he told her. 'The campers know it isn't anybody's fault—no one can predict an English summer, after all. We all have to be optimistic about it. It's up to us to organize plenty of indoor entertainment on bad days for the campers—we're rushed off our feet then, of course, for when the sun shines the campers are content to laze in the sun or swim or go for walks. But when it rains—' he whistled soundlessly. 'Indoor games and competitions, tea dances, amateur talent concerts, film shows . . .' He laughed. 'Then we wonder why we haven't enough staff to cope!'

'Only nine more days!' Gail sighed. 'Then the season starts.'

Johnny smiled. 'The first two or three weeks are usually very quiet—wait until July and August when we couldn't find a bed for one more person! Next week will go very quickly too, Gail—the rest of the boys and girls will trickle in—the resident staff, that is. A lot of our waiters and waitresses are locals—so are the band boys and the cleaning women . . .' He broke off suddenly and stared through the window intently. 'There's Tony in his car! I wonder what he's doing in Midleigh today. I'll hail him and get him to have some coffee with us.' Before Gail could speak, he had leaped up from the table and strode purposefully to the door.

Tony was looking for a parking place, cruising slowly down the High Street, so he very quickly spotted Johnny. He raised a hand in greeting and then pulled up. Johnny hurried over to him. 'Come and have coffee with us?' he invited.

Tony looked past him at the café window and saw Gail sitting at the table, her eyes upon the two men. He nodded. 'All right. I'll just park the car—be with you in a minute.'

Johnny rejoined Gail and ordered fresh coffee. It had just been served when the door was thrust open and Tony strode in, wrenching off his raincoat. He hung it up on the nearby stand and then slid into the seat next to Johnny.

He nodded to Gail. 'Lovely weather for

ducks!' he said drily.

She smiled coolly, studying him with a critical eye, noting the rumpled dark hair, the arrogant good looks, the casual way he wore his clothes, the long-fingered, sensitive hands which tapped restlessly now on the table before him. Johnny pushed the cigarette packet towards him. 'Have a cigarette? What are you doing in town, Tony?'

He shrugged. 'Picking up some goods—if I'd known you were coming in, I'd have asked you to save me a journey.'

'It's Johnny's day off,' Gail reminded him.

He threw her a quick glance. 'I know that.'

'As if that matters!' Johnny said swiftly. 'You know I'd have gladly picked them up if I'd known—why didn't you Tannoy me?'

Tony flicked his lighter into life and inhaled on the cigarette he had at last taken from Johnny's packet.

'It's a slack day,' he said through blue-grey cigarette smoke. 'The drive didn't hurt me.' He stirred his coffee and then drained the cup's contents swiftly.

Gail eyed him with dislike, wondering why she had ever imagined he possessed charm and good manners. Then a trace of compunction smote her. His hands still moved restlessly and there was a hint of strain in his handsome face, faint shadows beneath the dark eyes. She wondered if he were tired. It had been a busy time for everyone and Tony had a reputation

56

for hard work. Although Sunday was his official day off, he seldom left the camp and was always to be seen on Sundays, either in his office or about the grounds, doing more than his fair share of the organizing, always in demand.

Gail had seen him frequently about the camp, sometimes with a sheaf of papers in his hand, sometimes talking with animation to one or other of the staff; or dashing into the white-painted Office Block in search of Blair, demanding files, figures or schedules from Gail, insisting on immediate discussion on this, that or the other with Howard or Clare Marshall; arguing with Johnny over details of entertainment organization or sounding this or that person on new ideas. Always living up to the name which Howard had given him— Tireless Tony, Backbone of Blair!

Now he said abruptly: 'Ann's arriving tomorrow, Johnny. Will you find the time to pick her up at the station, do you think?'

Johnny frowned a little. 'What time?'

'Three-twenty at Combleigh,' Tony answered. He smiled briefly at Gail. 'Your chalet-mate,' he enlightened her. 'She's sweet on Johnny— so watch your step!'

Gail flushed angrily and glanced at Johnny. He was grinning broadly and she realized that it must be a familiar joke in the camp. Before she could frame a crushing retort, Tony rose to his feet in one swift, almost graceful movement for a man so tall and broad.

'I'm a busy man,' he said lightly. 'Have a good time, children!'

The door of the café slammed behind him.

Johnny leaned back in the wooden settle seat and put his head on one side. 'I have a strange feeling that there's no love lost between you and Tony Sheppard,' he said slowly.

'You don't have to be psychic to know that!' she snapped swiftly.

He ignored her retort. 'I wonder why?' he mused, almost to himself. 'Have I failed to emphasize to you what a splendid fellow he is?'

'I form my own opinions!' Gail said firmly.

'But we can't have hostility in the camp,' Johnny teased lightly. 'You two obviously haven't had time to find out each other's good qualities—I shall have to remedy that!'

She laughed reluctantly into his pleasant face. 'At the moment, I'm a busy woman,' she mocked him. 'My time is taken up with getting to know your good qualities!'

He grinned. 'Oh, I'm very easy to read—an open book! I wear all my good points on the surface. But Tony now—he's a different matter. He's very much a lone wolf, you know—reserved and possibly lonely underneath his charm and warm manner.'

She gave up. 'You're evidently a Tony Sheppard fan,' she said.

She waited while he paid the bill, then they left the café together. He tucked her hand in his arm and said: 'Look, the rain's stopped. Do you want to walk to the cinema?' She nodded and they set off. After a few minutes, he said: 'You're not worried about Ann, are you?'

She looked surprised. 'Why should I be?'

He shrugged. 'I meant what Tony said.' He smiled down into her small face. 'She's not really sweet on me—it's just one of the staff jokes. It's Tony she cares about, I think.'

'Oh, I see,' Gail said slowly and wondered why she felt a stab of resentment at this piece of information.

'Ann's a very nice girl,' Johnny went on. 'I'm sure you'll like her—she's full of fun and very pretty.'

'What does she do?' Gail asked.

'Works in Reception—you know, greets the campers when they arrive, answers their questions, is generally helpful—she's very popular.'

Gail nodded, and decided to reserve her opinion until she had met Ann Mathers.

The following evening she returned to her chalet when the day's work was done to find Ann busily unpacking, hanging her dresses in the wardrobe, and talking to Johnny who was sitting on Gail's bed.

'Here's Gail!' Johnny announced as she entered, and Ann turned quickly from the wardrobe. The two girls studied each other for

59

a moment then Ann smiled.

'Hullo, Gail!' she said warmly. 'I hope I'm not hogging the wardrobe.'

Gail shook her head. Johnny said quickly: 'I was just asking Ann if she brought some brighter weather with her. We're all fed up with this rain, aren't we, Gail?'

Gail threw her raincoat on a chair. 'That's an understatement,' she said lightly.

Ann slammed her suitcase shut and thrust it under her bed. 'I'm not unpacking any more for the moment,' she announced. 'Give me a cigarette, Johnny, will you?' He obediently produced a packet and handed them to her. Ann sat on the bed and curled her feet under her. 'How nice it is to be back,' she said with a contented sigh. 'I miss this place all winter.' She smiled at Gail. 'It grows on you!'

Gail returned the warm smile. 'I've already noticed that,' she said lightly. She crossed to the dressing-table by her bed and picked up a comb which she ran through her dark curls. Ann and Johnny began to talk, catching up on the news, exchanging their different ways of spending the winter. Gail listened absently, studying Ann unobtrusively as she moved about the chalet, tidying up after her new room-mate.

Ann broke off a spirited recital to say: 'I'm an awfully untidy person, Gail, I'm afraid.'

'That's all right,' she returned lightly. 'I'm very tidy myself—I don't mind doing this sort of thing.'

'You'll be doing it all the time with Ann,' Johnny warned her.

Gail smiled and went on with what she was doing.

Ann's auburn hair was long and silky, rich in colour, and straggling untidily over her shoulders at this moment. She had the creamy pallor of skin usual to auburn-haired people and a faint smattering of freckles across her snub nose. Her eyes were grey-green and fringed by long, dark lashes. She was tall and slender and self-possessed, yet Gail was conscious of a warm friendliness which emanated from her and she could understand why Johnny had said she was popular with the campers. She had a merry smile, a quick wit, bright eyes and a gay heart. Gail was relieved to find that she had formed a ready liking for Ann—it would have been impossible to live in close intimacy with her otherwise.

They drew Gail into the conversation and very soon she was perfectly at her ease with Ann, as they talked and laughed like old friends. At last, Johnny reluctantly rose to his feet. 'Tony will wonder where the devil I am,' he said. 'I'll see you later, girls.'

When he had gone, Gail drew the curtains and switched on the light. She began to unbutton her suit, for it was nearing dinner-time and she wanted to wash and freshen up.

'He's a nice person,' Ann said warmly, still

reclining on her bed, legs drawn under her, her long fingers twining a tress of her hair.

Gail slipped her coat across the back of a chair and turned on the hot taps at the wash-basin. 'Johnny? Yes,' she agreed.

'So you're Blair's new secretary? Well, let's hope you're more popular than the last one,' Ann said with a smile.

Gail had heard plenty about Susan Blake, and now she said sharply: 'At least I won't chase Tony Sheppard like she did!'

'You'll be wasting your time if you do.' Ann said smoothly. 'He's immune to women . . .'

Gail made no reply to this, and after a moment Ann got up from the bed and made an effort to tidy the chest of drawers which she had claimed.

While she washed, Gail wondered if Ann's words were really true. Was Tony immune? He seemed to like feminine company, but she had no proof that it ever went deeper than liking— quite the opposite, in her experience, she reminded herself bitterly and once again regretted that fate had thrown them together in such a fashion when she had taught herself to think of him calmly as a youthful infatuation . . .

CHAPTER SIX

Ann was a chatter-box. She admitted it freely and made no effort to check her lively tongue. It was one of the reasons for her popularity, for she was never unkind or malicious—her remarks were usually intelligent or gay and she brightened even the dullest day with her bright humour and easy optimism.

On the first day back at the camp she gave the lie to the tag that red-heads couldn't wear yellow. With her silken hair bound into a sleek knot at the back of her head, her lovely face discreetly made-up, she made an attractive picture in the grey skirt and yellow sweater. But she gazed appreciatively at the neat blue suit which Gail had chosen to wear and her eyes were vaguely envious. She had some lovely clothes of her own hanging in the wardrobe and Gail shrewdly assumed that on her day off Ann would make the most of her opportunity to wear them and would also prove her claim to popularity by enjoying herself, not only with the staff but also those campers who sought her company—for Ann had a healthy disregard for rules.

Gail quickly learnt all there was to know about Ann, for she had the candour of all talkative people—on only one point was Gail doubtful. Whether it was true or not that

Ann's affections were centred on Tony Sheppard.

He seemed very pleased to see Ann again—as indeed he was. He had always liked her open friendliness, the easy *camaraderie* she adopted with him, the complete lack of coquetry in her approach. He admired her efficiency, her poise, her handling of the campers, her zest for living and the gaiety which brightened any company. He welcomed her with a sincere warmth in his eyes and smile. She teased him with the usual jest—asking him lightly if he had enjoyed the winter at Blair—for it was a camp joke that Tony could never tear himself away from the place at the end of the season and remained to work through the winter, preparing the camp for yet another season.

Several new faces appeared during the next few days and Gail quickly lost track of all the newcomers. A few of them were introduced to her, but they were unimportant, for she had already made the friends who would see her through the summer—Ann, of course, and Johnny—a few of the others who had been at the camp when she arrived. The others would be likeable and friendly acquaintances—someone to exchange a laughing remark with or a casual nod or a mild grumble about this and that.

Thursday came around again. Johnny had said nothing to her about going together to

Midleigh, but Gail hoped they would again share a few hours of companionable intimacy.

She heard her name called as she left the staff dining-hall after breakfast and turned eagerly. Her uncle was hurrying towards her.

'Gail,' he said as he reached her side. 'I'm going to play truant for a day—my last chance for a few months, I expect. Would you like to come to London with me?'

Only a brief hesitation then she said quickly: 'Oh, yes! By car?'

He nodded. 'Of course. It won't take long—we can have lunch and do a matinée perhaps.' He smiled down at her eager face. 'It will be rather fun escorting a pretty girl again.'

She laughed. They turned and walked on and she linked her hand in his arm. 'It will be fun having you for an escort,' she assured him. 'I don't get the chance to go out with a handsome man very often.'

'Distinguished would be a better word,' he teased. 'I'm getting too old to be called handsome, you know—especially when I have such competition in those two!' He indicated Tony and Johnny who were standing outside the Main Building, talking and smoking cigarettes.

'I always preferred older men, anyway,' Gail returned smartly, smiling up at Howard.

His laugh pealed out and Tony turned at the sound, saying something to Johnny. They waved to Howard and Gail. 'You run along and put something cool on,' her uncle told Gail. 'The forecast is very promising—and it will be much warmer in London, I expect.' As she began to hurry off, he called after her: 'But bring your raincoat in case, Gail—one never knows!'

She smiled and nodded and then continued on her way. Howard walked over to join his Organizers.

'I'm going to London for the day,' he told them, accepting the cigarette which Tony offered. 'You won't need me—I hope!'

'Business?' Tony asked, flicking his lighter into flame.

'No—pleasure for a change!' Howard retorted. 'If anything crops up,' he went on 'you can handle it if anyone wants me, I've fled the country with the funds!'

A few minutes later, he strode off. Tony and Johnny exchanged glances. Then Johnny said ruefully: 'I think he must be taking Gail with him.'

'I had the same impression,' Tony agreed. 'Does that spoil your plans, by any chance?' A grin spread over his handsome face.

'I'll say! I bought some tickets for a dance in Midleigh—I thought it would make a change from the flicks and Gail told me she loves dancing.' He shrugged his shoulders.

'Take Ann,' Tony suggested. 'She enjoys dancing too.' He dropped his cigarette end to the ground and put his foot on it. 'You get on very well with Gail, don't you?' he said casually.

'Yes, I do. She's a grand girl—I'm very fond of her.' There was a trace of defiance in his tone.

'Don't you find her rather overwhelming?' Tony asked.

Johnny looked at him in surprise. 'What a funny thing to say,' he said. 'How do you mean, anyway?'

Tony shrugged. 'Just an impression—she always seems to be hanging on your every word . . . Don't you think she makes it very clear that she likes you?'

'What's wrong with that? I'm glad she does,' Johnny retorted. 'I hate these girls who run hot and cold—you never know where you are with them! One minute they think you the eighth wonder of the world—the next, they look you over as though you're something that came in with the cat!'

Tony chuckled. 'Well, if Gail thinks you're the eighth wonder, old man, she's going to have a shock one of these days. I gave her a warning the other day—but she didn't seem to take the hint. Perhaps I ought to make it more clear that you're just enjoying her company until something better comes along.'

Johnny flushed a little. 'It's different this time,' he said slowly. 'I'm really fond of Gail— I'm not anticipating any changes for a long while.'

Tony put his hand on his friend's shoulder for a brief moment. 'Sorry if I riled you,' he said shortly. 'But I've seen it happen so often with you . . . Not that I blame you, Johnny—I believe in steering clear of any long-lasting attachment myself.'

Johnny nodded his acceptance of the apology. He looked down at the cigarette he held between his fingers. It was burning low now and after a moment he dropped it to the ground and trod on it. 'You think Gail is getting serious?' he asked oddly.

'I think she's the type of girl who needs very little encouragement to get serious,' Tony replied. 'You know what I mean—the impetuous, romantic type—looks at a man twice and starts hearing wedding bells.'

Johnny looked at him sharply. 'That isn't the first time you've sneered at Gail,' he said. 'Why don't you like her?'

'I've hardly given her a thought,' he retorted. 'I don't know her well enough to decide if I like her or not.'

'In my opinion, you don't mean to get to know her,' Johnny told him.

'Any reason why I should?'

'No,' Johnny admitted reluctantly.

Tony grinned. 'I've told you—I always avoid the romantic type!'

'I think you're wrong about Gail,' Johnny said stoutly. He had his own opinion and nothing Tony said would shake it. 'I'd like to know what you base your ideas on, anyway.'

'Just an impression,' Tony repeated.

There was a pause. Then Johnny said lightly: 'I wonder if Ann would like to go dancing with me? We used to have some fun together last summer.'

'Sure you did! Don't get the reputation of being a one-woman man, Johnny—it wouldn't suit you!' Tony aimed a mock blow at Johnny's chin with a doubled fist and then turned away and entered the Main Building.

Johnny looked after him for a moment and then shrugged. He turned away and sauntered to the edge of the swimming-pool where he stood looking down into the water, bluer than any sea because of the deep-blue tiles which paved the bottom of the pool. His hands deep in the pockets of his slacks, he was very thoughtful. He did not believe that Gail was falling in love with him, despite Tony's warning. There were times when he sought a greater warmth and felt rebuffed by her immediate withdrawal: he knew that he was himself growing romantic about Gail. She had made a deeper impression on him than any woman before and though he would not commit himself to the thought that he loved her, he knew that his feeling for her was very akin to it and could easily develop. But his instinct told him that Gail had never thought of loving him: he was a good friend, a likeable companion. He doubted if it would ever be any more than that to Gail.

With a philosophical shrug, he walked away from the pool and went in search of Ann. He found her sunbathing in front of her chalet in shorts and sun-top, cigarettes by her side, a book in her hand.

'What's all this?' he demanded with mock severity.

She laughed up at him. 'You know we all ease off at the end of this week, Johnny. Don't worry, we'll have plenty to do on Saturday—and I'll be one of the hardest worked!'

He dropped to the grass beside her. 'Blair's gone off to London,' he said. 'While the cat's away . . .' He helped himself to one of her cigarettes.

'Do have a cigarette,' she said sweetly. He grinned broadly. 'Are you waiting for Gail?' she went on.

He raised an eyebrow. 'Should I be?'

'Aren't you going out together? She said only yesterday that you took her to Midleigh two weeks running.' She broke off. 'Have I said something wrong?' she asked quickly.

'No,' he assured her. 'It's quite true. Our days off happen to coincide. Where's Gail now?'

'She dashed back here to make a quick change—I thought she'd gone to find you. She went a few minutes ago.'

Without thinking, Johnny replied: 'She's gone with Blair—a better offer, I guess.' He turned his cigarette in his fingers. 'If you're intending to have a lazy day, anyway, Ann—why not have it with me? I've got some tickets for the Midleigh Town Hall dance—if you'd like to come?'

She smiled at him. 'Second-best? No, I don't mean that, Johnny. Thanks—it should be fun!' She wrinkled her forehead. 'Don't tell me that Blair is cutting you out? I thought Clare Marshall was more his type of person than Gail!'

Johnny hesitated. Howard had made it very definite that he wanted the relationship between himself and Gail to be kept a strict secret—and no one knew better than Johnny how quickly the news would get round if he mentioned it to Ann. She would not deliberately betray a confidence, but there were occasions when she thoughtlessly rattled on. So he merely said lightly: 'Every man likes variety, you know. Anyway, Gail is his secretary—he'll probably talk business all day. He can never forget the camp for long!'

In which he was wrong. For Howard found so many other subjects of conversation with his youthful niece that he did not mention the camp once. She greeted everything with such enthusiasm and was so prettily charming to him that he was very pleased that the idea of taking her along had occurred to him. He had always been fond of Gail and since she had been working for him they had grown much closer. The uncle-niece relationship was almost forgotten and she had easily become accustomed to calling him by his given name.

They talked a great deal about her mother and once or twice unshed tears sparkled in her eyes, for Gail still missed her mother very much. Howard soon understood how devoted she had been and how much she had done for her sick mother and this endeared Gail to him even more.

'You never liked Daddy, did you?' she asked at one time and Howard was startled by her perspicacity, for on the several occasions when he had visited them he had always hidden his dislike of Hubert Anson for Mary's sake.

Now he said disarmingly: 'Well, we never had very much in common, Gail.'

'I guess that does make a difference,' she agreed readily. 'He doesn't have many real friends, you know. People he plays golf with at the Club—but I don't think they're friends. The ones he used to have he dropped when he started making money—and I think his friends now rather despise him in their hearts because he was once a poor man . . . Isn't it strange how other people resent it when a man is successful?' she asked. 'Daddy has been very successful—but they sneer at him for being a self-made man!'

Howard nodded without committing himself. He said, with his eyes on the road ahead: 'How is he managing without you,

Gail? You used to run everything, remember.'

'After Mother died, Daddy decided we should have a housekeeper,' she told him. 'I'd made up my mind that I wanted to get away from home and do something with my life—he was all in favour of it. She's a very nice woman and very capable—a widow with two small children.'

'Your father won't mind that—he always liked children,' Howard said.

A pause, then she said slowly: 'I suppose he's young enough to marry again. Do you think he will, Howard?'

He shrugged. 'Why not? I imagine that Hubert is the kind of man who likes to have a wife—and next time he'll probably choose someone efficient and decorative to act as hostess to all his wealthy friends.'

She nodded. 'Joyce would fit that bill,' she said slowly. 'That's the housekeeper.'

'Would you mind a stepmother?' he asked with a smile.

'It wouldn't affect me very much,' she said honestly. 'I'm twenty-two now, Howard—I suppose I shall get married one day. I doubt if I'll ever live at home again for very long. If Daddy was happy—' she shrugged. 'That's all that matters, isn't it, Howard?'

'That's all that matters,' he agreed, approving of her common sense. How considerate and sensible she was, he thought to himself: so much more mature than she seemed on the surface.

They had a most enjoyable day in London. An excellent lunch in a famous Piccadilly restaurant; a stroll in the park; then a theatre. Howard was fortunate enough to get really good seats for a new musical show which they both enjoyed. The matinée was not possible on a Thursday so they caught the early show. Dinner at another restaurant and then the drive through the country back to Combleigh. Home again, Gail was pleasurably tired but satisfied with the day's outing and she kissed Howard good-night with affectionate warmth.

As she ran off to her chalet, he looked after her with tenderness in his expression and he thought that if he had married he might have had a daughter very like Gail.

Despite his great love for the camp, which was as dear as a child to him, he suddenly felt that his life had been empty without love, marriage and the prospect of flesh-and-blood children. Walking slowly towards his bungalow, he found envy in his heart of Hubert Anson— envy of at least one of his possessions.

CHAPTER SEVEN

There was a great bustle in the camp, for the first of the holiday-makers had arrived and Reception was more than busy coping with them.

Gail was seated at the desk, checking booking slips, taking payment, handing out chalet keys, marking her lists. There were four booths marked clearly with the four divisions of the alphabet—A–E, F–K, L–R and S–Z. As the campers arrived, they went to the booth which was applicable to the initial of their surname. This simplified matters a great deal, but it was still hard work.

Tony, Johnny and Ann were greeting them as they arrived and ushering them to their respective booths or answering eager questions.

Gail found the prevailing spirit very infectious and she returned the cheeky repartee which some of the campers threw at her with a ready wit and a laughing glance. During a brief pause, she thought about the busy intake and remembered what she had been told about the early season being easy compared with later in the summer. She could not imagine it being any busier than it was now, but admitted that this was probably because it was her first experience of the work and it was hard to keep cool and composed.

She welcomed her lunch break when it came. Tony approached the desk and said: 'There won't be any more now for an hour, thank goodness. The next train doesn't get here until two-thirty. We're going to lunch now, Gail.'

'Supposing some of them arrive by car?' she asked.

'We do allow for that kind of emergency,' he said drily and she flushed up at his tone. 'Linda will take over until we get back.'

She made no reply, gratefully rising from the desk. The girl he had mentioned came into the office.

'Pretty hectic for you on your first day,' she said in a friendly tone. 'But British Transport is very considerate, really—there's a whole hour without any trains pulling into Combleigh, between one and two-thirty!' She sat down in the chair next to Gail. 'Gives you poor creatures a chance to eat, anyway. We only get a few stragglers about this time and I can cope with them.'

'What about the alphabetical system?' Gail asked.

Linda laughed. 'I've got long arms,' she retorted. 'I sit here and stretch out for the other lists.'

Gail laughed too and left her. When she left the Reception Building she found Tony waiting for her, to her surprise.

'Johnny and Ann have gone on,' he said casually.

'There was no need for you to wait,' she told him coldly. 'I know the way to the dining-hall.' She began to walk on, but he caught her arm.

'As I did wait, we can walk together,' he said firmly and she had to slow her pace to his. He glanced down at her and smiled to himself. She looked directly ahead, her lips set, her chin raised just enough to be noticeable. 'You've been a bit rushed,' he said conversationally. 'But you'll soon get into the swing of things.'

'Of course I will,' she said.

'Of course you will,' he agreed and the smile broadened into a grin.

She fumed at his teasing and asked herself again why she had ever liked this over-confident, boorish and detestable man! But as they walked along the concrete paths he received many a greeting from campers and he had a smile and a quick word for them all. She could not doubt his popularity, but she reminded herself that these people only knew his superficial charm and their acquaintance was very short-lived—a few brief days and then they went away, to forget all about him until another year came round.

Suddenly he said: 'If you take offence at every remark I make to you, Gail, you'll go through the season perpetually annoyed with me.'

77

'If you were to treat me with as much respect and consideration as you treat the others, I wouldn't have to take offence,' she flashed back at him smartly.

'Respect? Consideration? Them's new words in these here parts,' he told her, grinning. 'I don't differentiate between anybody, my dear girl.'

She stopped short and her eyes were accusing.

'You're nice enough to Ann or Hazel or Linda,' she snapped. 'But you only speak to me to give orders or to be unpleasant!'

He took her arm again and drew her on. His eyes were suddenly hard. 'We don't like scenes between the staff, Gail,' he told her coldly. 'It gives the campers the wrong impression—and it spoils the happy, friendly atmosphere.'

'Don't be so pompous!' she sneered.

A passing camper caught the words and turned quickly, puzzled, startled by the sharpness of her tone. Tony swiftly remedied the situation by swinging Gail up into his arms and striding towards the pool. 'Any more cheek from you, my girl—and in you go!' he threatened her loudly in mock warning. The camper began to laugh and a few others were attracted by the scene.

'Throw her in, Tony,' one of them called. 'The first wetting of the season.'

Tony instantly dropped Gail to her feet and swung round swiftly to grab the camper who had spoken, a young boy in swimming trunks and sweater.

'So that's how you'd treat a lady?' he demanded. 'I think you should be the first one in the pool this season, my lad!'

The boy struggled, laughing, a little fearful that Tony meant to carry out his threat. Tony continued the play, pretending to drag the boy closer to the pool while all the time keeping his strong body between him and the water. Gail watched scornfully from the distance, but she was impressed by Tony's quick handling of the situation. The campers were urging him on to duck the boy: the boy's friends were encouraging him to throw Tony into the water instead. Suddenly, the boy jerked sharply, Tony lost his footing and shot into the pool, cleaving the water with his lithe body. He came up, shaking his dark head, striking out for the side. Well-pleased with the result, the campers turned back to their original pursuits and the boy ran off to join his friends.

Soaked, Tony stood on the edge of the pool, wringing out his sweater, apparently unperturbed by his ducking—the first of many that summer, as he well knew.

He walked over to Gail. 'Go and have your lunch,' he said curtly. 'Or you'll be the next in the pool!' This time it was no idle threat for the benefit of the campers.

Gail looked at his grim face and realized that beneath his display of coolness he was very angry. 'I'm sorry, Tony,' she said quickly.

He brushed back his wet, dark hair. 'Think nothing of it,' he said drily. 'I enjoy a swim before lunch—particularly when I'm dressed!'

Resenting his ungracious reply to her apology, she turned on her heel and walked away. He hurried after her. 'Next time you have any complaints, bring them to me in private,' he told her.

Gail threw him a furious glance and stalked off in the direction of the dining-hall.

Tony hurried to his chalet to change into dry clothes, meeting with not a few chaffing remarks on the way. In his chalet, small, comfortable and tidy enough to please even Gail, he stripped off his wet sweater and slacks and rubbed his lean, brown body with a rough towel. His anger faded very quickly and he was smiling to himself as he pulled on dry clothes. It would be all round the camp very quickly that the Chief Organizer had been the first ducking of the summer and he resigned himself to a good many leg-pulls, but he welcomed this and responded readily to them. He had been very tempted indeed to give Gail a ducking, but it was a strict rule of the camp that no girl was ever thrown into the pool and if campers attempted it they were quickly and firmly stopped.

Tony had to admit to a grain of truth in Gail's accusation. He had avoided her as much as possible since she had been at the camp and he had deliberately treated her coldly, not wishing to encourage her as fatally as the last time. He firmly believed that she was a romantic type of girl, as he had warned Johnny Greer, and Tony was a lone wolf who wanted no entanglements in life. He had no place in his future for a wife. As for love—he shrugged his broad shoulders as he closed his chalet door behind him. He had been in and out of love so many times that he doubted if it were possible to know a lasting emotion for any woman . . .

He joined the others at lunch when they were half-way through the meal.

'What happened to you?' Ann demanded.

He threw a quick glance at Gail who was keeping her attention on the meal and had barely acknowledged his arrival. 'Didn't Gail tell you?'

'Only that you'd gone to your chalet to get something,' Johnny replied.

'Yes—to get dry,' he retorted. 'Some little devil pushed me in the pool!'

'It happens to all of us at some time or the other,' Johnny told him unsympathetically. 'What's the water like today?'

'Wet!' Tony gave the usual stock answer, but it still brought a laugh bubbling to Ann's lips.

'Poor Tony!' she commiserated. 'I hope you got your own back.'

He glanced at Gail. 'The wretch ran off,' he replied. 'But I shall catch the right culprit in time, don't worry!'

'Perhaps we could inaugurate a new competition,' Johnny suggested suddenly with a twinkle in his eye. 'The first camper to duck Tony every week gets a prize!'

'I should spend my entire life in the pool,' he responded lightly. 'Not such a good idea, Johnny—unless you were the duckee instead of me.'

'No, thanks,' said Johnny quickly. 'That brainwave died an instantaneous and painless death!'

During this repartee, Gail had made no comment. Even their humour failed to bring a smile to her lips.

Ann turned to her swiftly. 'Do you feel all right, Gail?' she asked concernedly.

'Yes,' Gail replied quickly. 'Just a little weary, I think,' she added honestly.

'Of work—or our feeble attempts at wit?' Johnny asked with a smile.

'Work,' she assured him.

There was a bustle and noise of crockery and cutlery in the dining-hall—an atmosphere of suppressed excitement among those campers who had already arrived and were eating lunch in the dining-hall. It was an excellent meal, as were all those provided at Blair, thanks to Clare Marshall.

Gail looked around the room with its many tables, the attractive wall murals, the waitresses who were attentive to the campers' needs, the long wall entirely made of glass which overlooked the attractive swimming-pool set high on its grassy surround. It was a warm day but the skies were overcast. Johnny said suddenly, 'Saturdays are always grey days—it's odd, isn't it? As though the weather is in sympathy with reluctant campers who have to leave us for their everyday routine life.'

Ann said quickly, 'You're quite right, Johnny. Campers always come and go on heavy, dull days such as this one—it never gives any clue to the kind of weather we can expect for the following week and I'm sure many campers must feel disappointed on their arrival, expecting a wet week ahead or very little sunshine, anyway.'

'Saturday is a depressing day,' Tony said. 'The worst day of the week.'

'It's our easiest day, remember,' Johnny put in.

'Not for us in Reception,' Gail countered. 'Or am I just overwhelmed by my first experience of it?'

'It's busy enough for you,' Tony returned, barely glancing at her. 'But it's pretty slack for Johnny and me. We usually spend our mornings drinking coffee and smoking endless cigarettes in the Main Building, exchanging farewells with those who are leaving, welcoming the few early incoming campers with a smile and a friendly word—waiting for the evening when the new week starts with a swing at the Get-Together Dance.'

'I should hate to be merely a camper,' Gail said slowly. 'This place seems to steal your heart very quickly—I think I should be very nostalgic for it after only one week here.'

'I don't know what your reactions are to hordes of people with one aim in common—to, enjoy themselves to the utmost for one brief week—but if you like people for themselves, then you'll find Blair much dearer to you by the end of the season,' Tony told her.

Johnny said quickly: 'Gail has a great liking and understanding for people *en masse*. To work in a holiday camp, one must have—you know that as well as I do, Tony.' He smiled warmly at Gail across the table.

Tony raised an eyebrow slightly as he took a cigarette from the packet that Ann offered. 'I haven't had time yet to find out as much about Gail as you seem to, Johnny.' The words were almost a sneer. 'But it seems to be unnecessary—if I'm ever in doubt about her likes or dislikes, I'll come and ask you.'

Resenting his tone, Gail flushed and was ready with an angry retort, but a camper paused by their table.

'Hi, Tony—Johnny! Nice to see you again.'

They returned the greeting. Tony grinned up at the man. His smile was engaging and sincere. 'Back again, eh?'

'Of course. I wouldn't go anywhere else but Blair.' He winked. 'I know where the prettiest girls in England are to be found every summer.'

'Exactly my reasons for coming here to work every year,' Tony assured him.

'Are we going to have decent weather this week?' the camper demanded. 'When I came last year the camp was flooded by rain.'

'We've made different arrangements for you this year,' Johnny assured him swiftly. 'We've booked the sun for the entire season.'

The camper laughed. 'I notice you've got most of the familiar faces here again, Tony.'

'We don't like changes,' Tony told him. He rose to his feet. 'We're as hard-worked as ever, too. See you around.' He strode away, his body signifying urgency.

The camper looked after him and there was both affection and respect in his gaze. Then he turned back to Johnny. 'This camp wouldn't be the same without him—or you, either, for that matter. You two do wonders for this place.'

Johnny shrugged. 'The camp itself is about the best in England. It would be just as popular with different organizers.'

The camper was adamant. 'I've been to plenty of camps in my time. This is the best— I'm with you there. But the friendly atmosphere is created by you and Tony.'

Gail went back to Reception. Ann walked with her as Johnny had slipped away on business of his own. Gail was quiet and thoughtful. She knew the two men were popular with the staff: she had been assured that they were loved and admired by the campers, but this was her first experience of such affection displayed openly by a loyal camper. She felt a stirring of pride because now she was associated with Blair Holiday Camp and she knew a brief emotion of possessive pride in Tony and Johnny and pleasure because she had seen different sides to their natures than the campers ever knew. She wondered if she would be jealous of their popularity. They would always be in demand and their company welcomed with glad cries and friendliness. She would see little of them during the weeks that were to come—and she resented her lack of opportunity to break down the cool, impenetrable barrier of dislike which Tony had raised. But she clung to the fact that she and Johnny shared the same free day and she hoped that they would be able to spend some of that free time together, for liking had grown readily into affection for the young, pleasant organizer.

CHAPTER EIGHT

That evening gave Gail her first sight of a happy holiday crowd getting to know each other. She was a little surprised with the ease and familiarity of the gathering. There was no formality, no typical English reserve, no embarrassment. People fell into conversation as naturally as if they had known each other all their lives. Very little information was exchanged between them—first names, ages perhaps, the town they came from. Anything else was unimportant. The young people perhaps emphasized the ease of atmosphere. Swiftly, they summed each other up or chose their partners for the coming week and likings were formed on sight.

A little bewildered, Gail stood to one side of the ballroom dais and watched the happy, jostling crowd on the dance floor. There were few expert dancers: many could dance quite well: some had never set foot on a dance floor in their lives. It did not seem to matter. Everyone joined in. The good dancers were tolerant of those who jigged unrhythmically to the music—smiles and quick wit were exchanged light-heartedly. The local band was very good and Gail was quick to acknowledge this. She had not had many opportunities for dancing in the last few years but she enjoyed it and envied the couples on the floor now, as her foot tapped to the dance tune. Her quick eye caught sight of Johnny with a young girl in his arms. He was laughing down at her and swinging her gaily around the corners, apparently unconcerned that her steps were slow and uncertain.

It was strange how quickly one became accustomed to noise, Gail thought idly. After the peace of her old home in the country and then the comparative quiet during the last few weeks when the camp had been empty apart from the few staff, she had expected her ears to be deafened by the buzz of conversation and laughter and music in the ballroom. At first she had been a little conscious of it—now she assimilated it with the general atmosphere and she felt a glow of pleasure at the obvious enjoyment of the people around her. One could surely never be depressed or unhappy for long in such surroundings.

Someone touched her on the shoulder and she swung round quickly. A tall young man smiled down at her. 'Are you dancing?'

The question was so oddly phrased that she smiled. 'Not at the moment,' she replied, thinking that it must be obvious.

He jerked his head towards the milling crowd. 'Care to risk your life?'

Gail nodded. 'Yes—if you're careful of my feet.'

He grinned and followed her on to the

polished dance floor. They danced in silence for a few moments, then she looked up and found him regarding her thoughtfully. Her quick glance seemed to disconcert him. He reddened a little and said abruptly: 'That badge you're wearing—you're not on the staff, are you?'

'Yes, I am, actually.'

'I thought you were on holiday,' he said and there was a definite trace of disappointment in his tone.

Gail smiled. 'One long holiday,' she told him.

'I wouldn't have your job for anything,' he said. 'A week of it is enough for me.'

'Don't you like it?' she asked swiftly, a pang of fear shooting through her. It surprised her to find that it mattered so much to her that a complete stranger should find anything to criticize in the camp.

He seemed taken aback by the question. He did not answer for a moment, concentrating on manoeuvring her between two couples who were carrying on an excited conversation as they danced. 'Of course I like it,' he replied at last. 'I've been here four years running. But I couldn't stand the monotony of it—the same things week after week and more or less the same people.' He shrugged. 'People are alike, aren't they, after all?'

'I suppose that's true,' Gail agreed, 'but this is my first experience of working in a holiday camp so I don't know yet if I shall find it monotonous.' She smiled up at him confidently. 'I don't think I will.'

The music came to an end. He stood for a moment with his arm still about her. 'It's a pity you're on the staff,' he said slowly. She looked up at him with inquiry in her eyes, puzzled. 'You're pretty,' he went on. 'We could have had some fun together this week—but the staff and campers aren't allowed to mix too much here.'

Gail flushed a little. 'Thank you for the dance,' she said quickly and with a brief smile she left him.

She went over to the bar and ordered a Martini. The bartender who served her smiled at her. 'Having a good time?' he asked easily.

Gail shrugged. 'Better than you are behind the bar,' she retorted.

Graham smiled again. 'Oh, it's all right tonight—plenty of money floating about the camp. I've been treated several times already. It's not so good by the end of the week, though—sometimes I have to buy my own drinks then.' He surveyed her for a moment through half-closed eyes. Then he leaned over the bar towards her, lowering his voice a little. He had a confident air. 'I always like a little fresh air when the bar closes. I thought of going for a spin in my car—how would you like to come with me? Do you like cars?'

Gail had known for a few days that Graham

was interested in her. She liked him well enough. He was tall, fresh-faced, attractive with a crop of rich auburn hair and candid grey eyes. She considered him for a moment. He looked trustworthy and he was certainly very good-looking. But she shook her head. 'Not tonight, Graham. I've been rushed off my feet all day and I'm whacked. I must have an early night. Thanks all the same.'

'Another night then.' He passed over her refusal lightly. He was patient and there were plenty of girls to choose from. He had a vantage point behind the bar. He could watch the dancers and note the pretty girls who interested him: he had plenty of opportunities to indulge in mild flirtation.

Tony came up to the bar behind Gail and ordered a light ale. He nodded to Gail. 'What do you think of it all?' he asked absently.

Gail felt sure that he was not really interested in her reactions. He merely felt compelled to speak and an organizer had to know all the opening gambits of conversation.

'Great fun,' she returned lightly, sipping her Martini.

'I saw you dancing just now,' he said, sorting out the right money to give Graham. The bartender moved away to another customer, determining to pursue Gail further another evening. 'What do you think of the band?'

'Very good.' She paused a moment and then thrust: 'Your next question must surely be:

"Do you come here often?" '

He looked at her quickly, sharply. Then he laughed, thinking of the invariable answer to that question, which was a stock joke in the camp. 'Sorry,' he said. 'I'm a little absent this evening, Gail.' He raised his glass and drank some of the beer. He looked across the big room, smiled an acknowledgment to someone who waved, spoke to a man who passed him on his way to the bar and then glanced down at Gail again. She looked pretty. Her dark hair gleamed in the lights and her cheeks were a little flushed. Her eyes were bright with excitement and her lips parted with something akin to expectancy. The blue dress she wore almost matched her eyes. 'Let's dance,' he suggested and the words surprised him. He had been thinking that it would be pleasant to dance with her to the tune that Paul was playing—one of his favourites—and the suggestion had slipped from him without conscious effort.

She moved eagerly towards the dance floor and he followed her. Gail glanced back to see if he were close behind her and there was an expression in her eyes which disturbed him. It reminded him too vividly of the eager emotions she had displayed three years ago when he had been compelled to be brutal in order to discourage her attentions and affections.

She slipped into his arms with an ease that

hinted at intimate relationship between them. Tony frowned as her hand tightened on his shoulder. He swept her into the throng of dancers on the floor. He felt sure that she did not realize how blatant was her impulsive friendliness. She was naturally affectionate and readily responsive to any overture of friendship—trusting and gullible. But he must school himself not to suspect depth of emotion in her every movement, every gesture, every inflection of her attractive voice. He must learn to accept her casually—as she gave of her warm personality casually and with ease.

He seldom danced unless with a girl who seemed to lack company or was obviously shy. He called these his duty dances. He invariably introduced the girl to a crowd of young people afterwards and knew she would be content for the rest of the week for the youngsters were friendly and tolerant. Gail was light and rhythmic in his arms. Their steps matched well and the band, seeing Tony on the floor, repeated the number which he liked so well. He acknowledged the gesture with a wave of his hand to Paul, the bandleader, who smiled and jerked his head in Gail's direction as if to commend Tony's good taste.

As Gail danced with Tony, it seemed that the years slipped away and she was again at Stella's house, dancing to the radiogram in Tony's arms, besieged with her youthful love for him, unconscious that she embarrassed and amused him by the intensity of her emotions. Her hand tightened again on his shoulder and she moved her slim body closer to him. He gave no sign that he noticed and a few minutes later the music came to an end. Then it was that Gail realized that they had not exchanged a single word while their bodies moved together in time with the music. She was about to thank him for the dance when a camper laid a hand on Tony's arm and drew him aside. Gail waited a few seconds, then, reluctant to seem possessive, she went back to the bar and picked up her drink. Graham winked at her as he turned to serve a customer and she smiled. Tony did not come back to the bar. He had gone with the camper across the ballroom and was now sitting with the man and his friends, talking animatedly. Gail knew he would not be there long. Someone else would claim his attention and he would be moving from group to group for the rest of the evening when he was not running the novelty dances.

She stayed by the bar for some time. Graham leaned over the bar and talked to her when he was not serving drinks. She received several admiring glances and the occasional smile from the other men behind the bar, but they did not intrude, assuming that Graham was making a play for Blair's new secretary and wondering whether he would succeed. He was noted for his success with women.

Graham did not have long to concentrate

on Gail. The bar was busy and several customers fell into conversation with her as they waited for their drinks. One young man bought her another Martini and stayed to talk with her for a while. Then he indicated a circle of his friends who sat around a table near the bar.

'If you're on your own, why don't you join us?'

Gail glanced in the direction of his friends. They were young and rather noisy but obviously enjoying the evening. She smiled. 'Yes, I will. Thank you.' She walked with him across to the table.

'My name's Roger,' he volunteered. 'Have you been to this camp before?'

She shook her head. 'My first time at any camp,' she told him.

'Is it really?' He seemed surprised. 'Well, we'll have to see that you enjoy it. Do you play tennis?'

'Yes.'

'Good. We must have a game,' he told her lightly. His friends glanced at her with interest as Roger paused by the table, his hand slightly touching her elbow as if to impress upon the crowd that he had already laid claim to the attractive girl by his side. He glanced down at the badge she wore to discover her name. If he noticed the word 'Staff' above it, he made no mention of it. 'You'll find our crowd a bit confusing at first, Gail,' he said, 'but I expect you'll soon get all the names right.' He rattled off a string of names, indicating the owner of each as he did so. 'This is Gail,' he finished.

One young boy leaped to his feet. 'Have this chair,' he offered. 'I'll get another one.'

She was a little touched by his ready courtesy and sat down obediently. They all accepted her without question or surprise and went on with their various conversations. Roger pulled up his chair until it was almost touching hers and smiled at her. 'Seems a good crowd this week,' he said lightly. 'Unexpected really, so early in the season.' He brought out cigarettes and offered them around. He turned back to Gail and went on: 'I always take one week of my holidays in May. With our English summers, one is just as likely to get good weather then as at any other time.'

The same boy who had given up his chair rose to his feet as the band struck up again. 'Will you dance with me, Gail?' he asked. He was fresh-faced, youthful and Gail placed his age as about sixteen. He had the boisterous eagerness of adolescence. She nodded gladly and got to her feet. The boy grinned at Roger. 'You don't mind if I dance with your girl, do you, Rog?'

Roger winced a little—whether at the question or at the abbreviation of his given name, Gail wasn't sure. He waved a hand lightly. 'Go ahead.'

Her hand held in a tight, rather hot clasp,

Gail went with the boy to the dance floor. He grinned down at her. Gail said quickly, 'Let me see—you're Stan, aren't you?'

He nodded. 'That's right.'

Gail noticed the badge on his blazer pocket and she said easily: 'Are you still at school?'

He flushed and seemed a bit put out at the question. 'Of course not!' he returned indignantly. 'How old do you think I am, then?'

Gail smiled. 'Seventeen?' she hazarded a little untruthfully. By the way he preened she knew that he was younger but complimented by her guess.

'Not quite,' he had to, admit and she admired his honesty. 'But I soon will be,' he added hastily. He surveyed her thoughtfully and then stumbled over her feet. He danced with the uncertainty of youth and the awkwardness of one unused to dancing. 'You're about seventeen too, aren't you?' he said.

Gail laughed. 'Good heavens no!' she retorted, and then hoped immediately that she hadn't sounded patronizing. 'I'm twenty-one,' she added quickly.

'Roger's only nineteen,' he hastened to inform her, as if anxious to wean her away from that young man.

'He looks older,' she replied. 'Did you all come together?' she asked a moment later with curiosity.

He shook his head. 'No. I came with Brian and Danny. Roger came with Tony, Terry and Bill. We all met up here—they seem all right. We'll have some fun this week—stir the camp up a bit.'

Gail looked a bit dubious at his words. But she did not put her instinctive fears into words. Instead she said: 'I shall be working in a stuffy office most of the week—but I'll keep an eye out for you all.'

'Working?' His voice was horrified.

'Yes. I'm on the staff here—didn't you see my badge?'

He shook his head again. 'Does Roger know that?'

Gail laughed. 'Does it make any difference to him then?'

'Of course it does. Roger's looking out for a girl to spend the week with—we all do. I've got my eye on one over there—she's only a kid, though. Nothing serious, of course. I've got a girl at home. But we all want a bit of fun. Roger will be choked . . .' The music stopped and he led her back to the table. As soon as they reached the crowd, Stan said loudly, 'Roger, you're out of luck after all. Gail works on the staff here.'

Roger looked quickly at Gail and his eyes apologized for his uncouth friend. She smiled with understanding and he relaxed. 'Lucky girl,' he merely commented and she sat down beside him. Ignoring Stan, he began to talk to

98

her and she found him to be intellectual and sensitive beyond his nineteen years. It was with some reluctance that she eventually left them all some time later. She had danced with Stan again and with Roger several times. The other boys in the crowd had danced with her and she had found their company enjoyable and amusing. But Johnny caught her eye and beckoned to her and she excused herself from them with a promise to 'see them around', the camp slogan which she had easily adopted.

Johnny slipped his arm about her shoulders. 'I see you're making friends already,' he said lightly. 'Bit young for you, though, Gail.'

'They're very sweet,' she defended quickly. 'The one I was talking to may be young, but he's very sensible and mature for his age.'

Johnny raised an eyebrow. 'I've competition, have I?' he said ruefully. 'Anyway, Gail, there's a party after the dance for the staff. Always on the first night of the season. It's usually good fun. You're not too tired to stick around, are you?'

Gail laughed. 'Not when there's a party in the offing.' She glanced at her watch. 'Eleven-thirty the dance ends, doesn't it?'

'Yes. Some of the boys have a skiffle group and the bar opens up again at midnight. We won't disturb the sleeping campers—the nearest chalets are too far away to be worried by the noise. I must rush off now, Gail—we're going to do a spot waltz and Tony needs me.

But promise me you won't slip away to bed—I want you at that party!' He smiled warmly at her, and she felt her heart lift a little at the obvious affection in his eyes. As he walked away, she looked after him and there was a faint unhappiness in her heart that Tony never looked down at her with such an expression lighting his dark, handsome features. His eyes were usually hostile when he glanced at her.

CHAPTER NINE

The weather was as surprisingly sunny and warm again and the campers made it no secret that they considered themselves very fortunate. It was a happy week. Gail had never been so contented and she woke every morning with a welcome in her heart for the new day.

Howard was very considerate and insisted that she should have a couple of hours off each afternoon in order to enjoy the good weather.

'You can work harder when it's raining,' he said lightly. 'But the sun shines so rarely in England that I want you to take advantage of it now. Run along and enjoy yourself, Gail—get some colour into those pretty cheeks.'

She tiptoed to kiss his chin affectionately. 'I must say that you make a wonderful boss, Howard,' she told him warmly. 'But I'll feel guilty lying in the sun and thinking of the work piling up.'

'Nonsense. You'll work all the faster after a break, my dear.'

He proved to be right, for when she reluctantly left the sun and her new-found friends to return to her desk, her nimble fingers and quick brain seemed to cope with the awaiting work without conscious effort on her part.

Days sped by on wings. In her free time Gail was with Roger a great deal. He seemed to like her and instinctively gravitated to her side as soon as she appeared in the midst of the campers. He was delighted to find that her tennis was good, for he played in the Junior Championships of his county and loved the game. She grew very fond of the crowd of young people. Although Stan was terribly young and brash, and often uncouth, she found it in her heart to sympathize with the difficulties of adolescence and to understand his sense of security which led to the need to be the centre of attraction. Away from the others, she found him to be sensitive and much quieter and a little unhappy. Roger told her lightly that Stan must bring out her maternal instincts when she told him this, and there was possibly a lot of truth in his words. They were a likeable set of youngsters with warm hearts and nothing was too much for any of them to do for Gail, whom they had taken into their midst with easy affection.

She spent every evening with them: dancing, talking, the occasional drink, playing snooker or table tennis when dancing bored, swimming in the pool after the dance ended, boating on the small lake which was wet but amusing, walking along the beach towards the cliffs with Roger on one side and Stan on the other, their arms about her, the crowd accompanying them as always. She seldom had a chance to talk to

Roger alone, but when she did she loved to listen to him. He was a great reader, a very intelligent young man, and an ardent lover of classical music. He had decided views on most subjects which he discussed with Gail at length, aided and abetted by his friend Terry. She found out many things about Roger during those few short days—very little from Roger himself, who was shy of talking about his background but would talk for hours on his interests—but from Terry, who had the greatest admiration for Roger.

Terry, although of the crowd, was not always with them in spirit. At first, Gail had been rebuffed by his expression of arrogance and superiority. He was tall, fresh-faced with blue eyes and blond hair. She discovered that he was an ex-public schoolboy of very good family. She also discovered that beneath his arrogant exterior pumped a very warm heart and a love of his fellow beings which he found difficulty in expressing. He often seemed aloof even in the midst of the noisy crowd—yet he could be as noisy and merry as any of them when he chose. He was the same age as Roger, but he had the poise and bearing of a much older man. Two friends had surely never been so dissimilar as these two boys, yet they shared an affinity which was evident even to the most disinterested observer. Gail preferred Roger and Terry out of the whole circle of young people and she was more often in their company. Despite Stan's words at the beginning of the week, Roger seemed quite content to seek her out in her few hours of free time during the day and perfectly happy to spend his evenings with her. No other girl seemed to interest him and Terry apparently found none to his taste at the camp, for he remained aloof and alone all week.

Ann teased Gail about her interest in the young men. 'They're years younger than you,' she said lightly. 'You're just a cradle-snatcher, Gail.'

'Two years,' Gail returned. 'That isn't so much and they're very mature. I like them, anyway.' She said this firmly and Ann, glancing at her quickly, decided not to pursue the subject.

'You're in a better position than any of us,' she said. 'Although you're staff, you're really quite free to wander about the camp with whom you like. I wonder that Blair hasn't taken you up on it before this. He usually discourages us from spending too much time with any particular camper. Of course, Tony and Johnny are always in the public eye and if they concentrated too much on one girl it would set the whole camp talking. But I'm sure that many of the campers aren't sure whether you're on the staff or on holiday.'

Gail smiled. 'It seems like one long holiday to me,' she retorted. 'I love it.'

As she had surmised, Gail saw little of Tony

or Johnny. They were always in demand. So many things needed their attention, for every hour of the day was organized for the campers' entertainment. She rarely had the chance to speak to them, although she saw them about the camp. They would wave or smile as she passed and Johnny occasionally gave her a quick word. She was surprised to find that Tony was popular with children. They had their own organizers, yet whenever Gail caught sight of Tony's tall, dark-haired figure, he invariably had a child on each hand and a few others close behind him clamouring for his attention. He was very patient and kind, and Gail felt sure that he spent most of his wages on sweets and ices for the children who followed him about the camp as though he were the Pied Piper.

Both organizers were conscious of Gail's presence about the camp. Her trim figure and proud head became familiar sights in ballroom or games room or playing field or around the swimming-pool. Her merry voice carried across to them or her light laugh tinkled out above the buzz of noise and activity.

Johnny welcomed the invasion of Gail in his thoughts and emotions. He no longer worried that he might be falling in love with her. He revelled in the spark of jealousy which burned when he watched her dancing in another man's arms or laughing at some joke or talking eagerly to one of the crowd of young people who had adopted her as one of themselves. He did not resent his full days which prevented him from spending much time with Gail, for he loved his work too much. He was content for the most part that she had made friends with the young crowd and reminded himself that they would be leaving the camp on the following Saturday and Gail would probably never see them again.

Tony scarcely thought about Gail, yet he surprised himself by waking up several times to the realization that he was watching her, waiting for her infectious laugh, hoping for a quick glance from her bright eyes. He then chided himself and thrust her from his mind, turning to his work with renewed zest and vigour. As the week drew on, he overheard one or two remarks thrown into the general pool of staff conversation which disturbed him. He shrugged them off at that time, but when he heard a crowd of elderly campers discussing the same theme, he decided it was time to have a word with Gail. He waited for the right opportunity, but it was surprising how seldom he seemed to see her about the camp now that he was consciously looking for her. Whenever he did, she was with one or other of the crowd of young people that she seemed to like so much, or she was hurrying from one place to another and it was impossible to catch her eye.

Johnny waited for Gail at the end of the dance on Wednesday evening. She came out of the ballroom with Terry and Roger, who were discussing whether to have an early night for once or to chance a swim. It was the coolest night of the week so far and Gail had already decided that she was not swimming in the pool that night. Johnny moved forward into the stream of light from the ballroom doors and spoke her name. Gail paused. 'Hallo, Johnny—did you want me?'

He took her arm. 'I won't keep you a minute—I only want to speak to you.'

Roger looked at Gail and then politely moved out of hearing, drawing Terry with him. The two boys stood on the edge of the lawn arguing in low tones. Johnny smiled down at Gail. 'I'm not interrupting anything, am I?'

'Don't be silly,' she said lightly. 'Of course not.'

'It's only about tomorrow. Our day off, remember? Have you made any arrangements yet?'

Gail hesitated. Terry and Roger had hailed the news with delight and all evening they had been discussing how they would spend the morrow. Because Johnny had not mentioned it to her until now, she had assumed that he meant them to go their own ways this week. Nevertheless, she had still not promised Roger that her free day would be entirely given up to the crowd and she was glad now of this.

'Nothing definite,' she said slowly.

'Good! Will you let me steal you from those

boys for one day, Gail? I should think you feel the need for adult company by now.'

He said the words lightly but Gail still wondered if they were meant to be a sneer and she felt a momentary irritation. She hesitated a little. Then she said, 'All right, Johnny. But I have promised to play tennis in the morning. Can we meet after lunch?'

He had made plans to take her out to lunch in Midleigh and then laze on the beach there for the afternoon. He said with a trace of disappointment in his voice, 'Well, I have to be back by six, you know. It doesn't give us very much time, Gail.'

'There isn't much to do anyway outside the camp,' she said.

'You *are* in love with the place,' he said, and immediately regretted the sharpness of his tone.

She treated his remark lightly. 'Of course I am. After lunch, Johnny?'

'Yes. I'll see you in the morning, anyway.' He turned away and walked briskly towards the staff chalets, aware that his back was hostile and wondering if she looked after him.

But Gail had joined Roger and Terry and linked her hand in Roger's arm affectionately. 'Made up your minds yet?' she asked.

'Yes. No swim tonight,' Terry replied.

Roger looked a little disturbed. 'Is that chap sweet on you?' he asked. 'Or is that a personal question?'

Gail chuckled. 'Who? Johnny? Of course not,' she returned lightly, but his question remained with her after she had left the two boys and gone off to bed. They always wanted to escort her to her chalet door, but, knowing the campers weren't allowed in the staff grounds, she always refused. Ann wasn't in the chalet and Gail undressed and prepared for bed in quiet solitude. She supposed that Johnny was 'sweet on her' in the modern interpretation of the vernacular. She knew he was fond of her and liked her company. But she was very fond of him too and was pleased that he wanted to be with her. It never occurred to her that his emotions might go deeper than light affection and now, remembering his odd reaction to her words only a short time ago, she was a little disturbed. But as she climbed into the coolness of her comfortable bed she brushed aside her fears and settled for sleep.

It seemed a long time before Ann arrived. Gail was just drifting into sleep when she heard Ann's low voice followed by a laugh. Gail roused and then stiffened as the distinct tones of Tony's voice reached her. The words were unimportant. It was the very fact that he was with Ann at such a late hour which was like a sword thrust to Gail's heart. She had never given Johnny's information about Ann's emotional preference for Tony another thought: now it came rushing back to torment her and she knew that she was jealous. She had always considered that she had a prior claim on Tony because of their previous association—but Tony had always made it clear that he preferred to forget the past and had no intention of taking any interest in her in the present.

Lying in the darkness, she listened to the murmur of voices and then the unmistakable silence which indicated an exchange of kisses between the two outside the door. Gail clenched her hands, not caring that her fingernails cut deep into the palms. The door was opened quietly and she heard Tony say: 'Don't disturb Gail.'

'I'll be as quiet as a mouse,' was Ann's reply and then she stumbled against a chair which clattered and she went into a torrent of laughter.

'That's enough to wake the dead—let alone Gail,' Tony said sharply.

Ann tiptoed over to Gail's bed, looked down at her supine form in the semi-darkness. Gail feigned sleep but cleverly moved a little as though restless after the unexpected clatter. Apparently satisfied, Ann turned away.

'It's all right, Tony,' she whispered.

'She must be very tired,' he returned. 'Well, good-night, Ann.'

'Good-night.' Ann shut the door quietly, switched on the light and regarded Gail for a moment or two. The bright light caused Gail's lashes to flutter and Ann smiled. 'I know you're not asleep,' she said lightly. 'Sorry I woke you, Gail.'

Gail opened her eyes and forced a smile to lips that seemed stiff and cold. 'I wasn't really asleep.' She rolled over to look at her watch. 'What time is it?'

'Later than I care to remember,' Ann said with a mock groan. 'I shall hate getting up in the morning.'

'Half-past two!' exclaimed Gail.

Ann moved about the chalet, preparing for bed. 'Tony and I went for a walk,' she volunteered. 'He had a headache and I wasn't a bit sleepy. Now I'm nearly dead.'

Gail settled down again to sleep. 'I've got to get up too,' she said. 'So I'm not going to talk to you until the crack of dawn.'

'It's your free day,' Ann reminded her. 'Lucky you! You can sleep as long as you like.'

It was a long time before sleep eventually cast its veil of peace over Gail. She listened to Ann's rhythmic breathing and envied her. Her thoughts were all of Tony and his warm personality, the dark good looks which attracted her so much, the depths to the man which so few people were privileged to know— perhaps Ann was allowed an insight into the real Tony and the thought brought pain. Gail dwelt on the cool and, she was sure, superficial façade Tony showed to her in the determination to prove that she had never meant anything to him in the past and that he was not interested in her now. Surely they could be friends at least? She would not make a fool of herself again and embarrass him with impulsive affection. But it was impossible to always be in such close contact with Tony and not feel the old attraction steal over her heart, not to want his friendship and liking. Tears ran down her cheeks. He apparently preferred Ann—and Gail was honest enough to admit that Ann was a lovely girl with a sweet nature and a fine cast of character. She had never given Gail any reason to think of her as promiscuous, so it was obvious that if she had stayed out with Tony until half-past two in the morning, then she must be very fond of him and undoubtedly he found her attractive. Did the secret lie in Ann's light manner and casual coolness which never betrayed her innermost feelings? Was it this that appealed to Tony— and explained why he had rebuffed Gail three years ago, because she had made her feelings too obvious? He seemed to like being a lone wolf in life and apparently avoided any emotional entanglement which went beyond friendship. But Gail knew that now, as much as ever before, it was impossible for her only to offer Tony friendship—she had never regained her heart and it was still in his keeping.

With her brain in turmoil and the tears still near to the surface, Gail finally slept but only to dream of Tony and Ann together and herself on the outside of the bond they shared.

CHAPTER TEN

Graham gave a low whistle of approval and Gail turned swiftly, the short skirt of her white tennis dress swirling.

Graham grinned at her and crossed the lawn to join her. 'Anyone for tennis?' he teased. 'I must say you look very decorative, Gail. I think I'd better start taking an interest in tennis.'

She laughed. 'I think indoor sports are more in your line.'

His eyes were still approving as he studied her. 'I must admit they're more enjoyable—with the right company. When are you going to try out my car?'

Her smile was coquettish, but she was not aware of the fact. 'Oh, one of these days.'

'I shall hold you to that,' he assured her. 'Do me a favour, Gail—I've got a message for Tony but I'm due on duty in three minutes. Will you see that he gets it? You'll be passing the ballroom and he's probably in his office right now.'

'Of course I will.' She took the slip of paper he held out to her. 'See you around, Graham.'

He nodded and watched her walk gracefully in the direction of the ballroom. His grey eyes approved the lithe swing of her slim figure, the short dark hair ruffled slightly by the gentle breeze, the unconscious poise of her bearing. He wondered if she were really as naïve as she seemed. He had frequently hinted at his interest in her, but she rarely responded to his attempts at flirtation. He had realized that it would need a more subtle approach to win Gail's friendship. He was not unduly worried by his repeated failure, for he was both patient and confident that one day she would not adroitly brush aside his invitation.

Gail looked for Tony in his office, but the small room was empty. There was evidence that he had recently been around—his fountain pen lay on the table with its cap off and he was the kind of man who had respect for his personal possessions. She knew he could not be far away.

She paused a moment outside the door, her hand still on the catch, scanning the long room for some sign of Tony. A camper hailed her. 'Looking for Tony or Johnny?'

She turned towards the woman who had spoken and walked across to where she sat. 'Tony. Do you know where he is?'

'Of course I do.' There was a faint contempt in the woman's voice for anyone who did not keep a constant track of the organizers' movements. Gail fought down a surge of irritation and repressed the impulse to remind the woman that she had other things to do than keep a close watch on Tony or Johnny. 'They're rehearsing for the concert,' the woman told her grudgingly. She indicated a door. 'If you go through there, you'll see the steps leading to the stage. That's where they all are.'

Gail thanked her briefly and slipped through the door. As soon as she did so, her ears were assailed by the rich quality of a man's voice who sang not only well but with love for music in the tones. She paused to listen. Then slowly she walked up the steps, very quietly, not wishing to interrupt the rehearsal, knowing a sense of pain that in a moment the beauty of the song would cease. Gail hesitated in the wings of the stage—the shock of discovering Tony to be the owner of such a voice took her breath away. She had never heard him sing and he was not the kind of man to broadcast his own assets. Listening to him and knowing that the wonder of his voice filled her entire being, she could forgive him anything—even the pain of the previous night. When the song ended, she moved forward on to the stage and Tony glanced at her. Their eyes met and held for a long moment. Then Gail held out her hand, offering the slip of paper. 'Graham asked me to give you this note,' she said, feeling at a loss and annoyed with her own lack of poise.

Tony nodded and took it from her. 'Thanks.' He moved across to the piano and bent his head over Nick, the pianist. He picked up a list from the top of the piano and they consulted it together, talking in low tones.

Several campers were on the stage, one or two talking together, others waiting to rehearse their act for the concert. One man shuffled his feet nervously, his face hot and his manner uncomfortable. Gail wondered if he had volunteered to appear in the concert or whether he had been persuaded against his will by friends or family. She smiled reassuringly at him and he moved across to her. 'You doing anything in the concert tonight?' he asked her, clearing his throat with a sharp jerk.

Gail shook her head. 'No talent,' she returned lightly.

He looked her over. 'I wouldn't say that,' he said and there was an over-familiar look in his eyes which disturbed her. 'What about the chorus, love?'

She flushed under his scrutiny. Tony came back to the centre of the stage. 'Right, everybody!' he said with authority in his tone and the man by Gail's side turned towards Tony to her relief. 'I shall want to run through a couple of sketches this evening before dinner,' Tony said easily. 'Otherwise, everything seems all right.' He referred to his list and grimaced. 'I'm just left with the difficult task of compiling the programme. Tony always gets the dirty work,' he added with a laugh that took the sting from the words. 'Perhaps you'd all turn up about five o'clock for a last run through in case there are any hitches?'

There was a murmur of assent, then the crowd began to disperse. There was a concerted movement towards the wings and the steps down to the ballroom. Tony grinned at Gail.

'I don't envy your job,' she said.

'Oh, it's not so bad. One concert is very much like another,' he told her. 'They aren't too bad a crowd for talent this week. Of course, we can really put on a good show later in the season—for the first few weeks, it's mostly staff talent.' He took her arm and they moved towards the steps after the campers. He glanced over his shoulder. 'Five o'clock, Nick? I'll leave you to sort out that arrangement.'

Gail said eagerly: 'I never knew you could sing like that, Tony. It was wonderful.'

He shrugged off the compliment. 'There have to be several sides to an organizer, you know.' He glanced down at her. 'Are you meeting anybody for the moment—or have you time for a cup of coffee with me?'

Surprised by his suggestion, she assented quickly. 'I'm due to play tennis soon—but I'll give you ten minutes.'

Tony smiled. 'Long enough.' He indicated one of the tables which were spaced about the cafeteria. 'Go and sit down, Gail—I'll fetch the coffees.' Within a few minutes he came over to her and placed two steaming cups of the

118

fragrant beverage on the table. He sat down and brought out his cigarettes. 'Well, what do you think of the camp now?' he asked.

She glanced at him with a mock threat in her eyes. 'Don't make conversation, Tony—or I shall forgo this delightful-looking coffee!'

Their eyes met briefly. 'I'm not just being polite this time,' he assured her, and she knew by the warmth in his tone that he was truthful. 'I really do want to know if you're happy here.'

Gail nodded and she laid her hand on his arm for a mere space of a second. 'Of course I am.'

'I wanted to talk to you,' he said and he paused awkwardly, as though uncertain how to phrase his next words. Gail looked at him inquiringly. 'Look here,' he went on. 'I'm not trying to interfere with the way you run your life—it wouldn't be any of my business anyway—but will you take some advice from me?'

She looked startled. 'It all depends on the advice.'

Tony nodded. 'I know you hold rather an exalted position here. Being Blair's niece, naturally you can get away with things that the rest of the staff can't—but you can't run around with the campers like you've done this week without being talked about—by staff and campers both.'

Gail stirred her coffee—and anger was stirring in her heart too. 'Talked about? I don't know what you mean.'

'Of course you don't. I doubt if you've heard any of the gossip.' He studied her flushed face. 'I'm probably leaving myself wide open for a heated argument with you, Gail—but that won't be anything new between us.' He smiled briefly. 'I'm not getting at you personally— please believe that. You're spending a lot of time with that crowd of youngsters— particularly the boys. I'm not suggesting there's any harm in it, Gail—but people will talk. You know the rule about staff mixing with campers—it's broken often enough by all of us, but we're careful not to push our luck. Well, you're pushing your luck a bit too far— and some of the staff are going to wonder why you aren't hauled over the coals. Will you promise me to be a little more selective in your choice of company for the rest of this week?'

Gail was angry. To prevent the swift rush of words, she lifted the cup of coffee to her lips and drank a little of the hot liquid. 'How dare people talk about my actions?' she demanded.

Tony shrugged. 'Human beings love an opportunity to criticize, Gail—be your age. They'll talk about anybody, innocent or otherwise, given enough reason. And you must admit you've given them reason this week. Every moment of your free time you spend with one or other of that crowd—and it's usually the one they call Roger. He's only a kid, that's obvious—it's also obvious that he's getting too attached to you and that isn't fair dealing on your part.'

'I didn't think people could be so petty.' Gail said harshly. 'My friendship with Roger and the others is perfectly innocent—they're nice youngsters and I'm very fond of them.'

'You make a habit of giving your affections impulsively,' Tony said slowly. 'That's up to you—but I should think more of your integrity if you gave a thought to the feelings of that young man. You're blatantly leading him on—and you know it!" he accused.

'Is that what people are saying?' The flush had died and Gail's face was deathly pale now. She did not care that there should be gossip about Roger and herself. They shared an innocent and heart-warming friendship and if people liked to misconstrue it because their minds and natures were too narrow to recognize that there could be such a friendship between a boy and girl, then it could not really affect either of them greatly. But Tony's reminder that she gave her affections impulsively hurt her—the thrust went deep and she had barely heard the rest of his words although the import was inescapable. She shrugged now. 'Do you think there's anything between Roger and me but friendship?' She knew that if he hesitated before answering and then lied to her she would never forgive him.

But Tony did not think for one moment that

her morals were at fault. He was convinced that she saw no harm in her liking for the young men or her wish to be constantly with them—and no doubt there was no harm in their thoughts of her. They were young and on holiday and Gail was probably an ideal companion. He said without hesitation: 'No, I don't. But I don't care to have you talked about all over the camp, Gail. It isn't pleasant. When you first came here I understood that you didn't want any preferential treatment—that you wanted your relationship to Blair to be kept secret and more or less forgotten by those who knew.'

'That's true,' Gail agreed, wondering what was coming.

'Therefore I must exercise my authority over the staff—and you come in that category, I'm afraid. I'm not asking you to break off with that crowd altogether—I'm not unreasonable, I hope. But don't give the gossips any more fodder. Those boys will be going home on Saturday—you'll never see them again. A friendship between any of you can't possibly last, so you lose nothing by choosing different company for the rest of the week.'

'I've already arranged to meet Roger again,' Gail said tightly. 'At the end of the season, I shall probably stay in London for a while. Roger and I are going to some concerts together.'

Tony pursed his lips. There was a firm

stubbornness in Gail's eyes which he feared to rouse completely. The lift to her chin betrayed determination. He had to go warily. She was not a child and, of course, was quite capable of choosing her own friendships. But he knew that gossip was rife in the camp—he had heard it himself and had some of it repeated to him. He might not hold any particular brief for Gail, but he did object to having her name linked with slanderous suggestions. 'The end of the season is a long way from now,' he reminded her gently. 'There'll be lots of nice young men like Roger coming to the camp for one week whom you'll like and hope to see again one day. Gail, I've tried to impress this upon you before. Friendships spring up quickly here—and they're soon forgotten on both sides. You must remember that you're only ships passing in the night—live for the present.'

Gail laughed scornfully. 'I am living for the present. I found out long ago that planning for a future with anyone doesn't pay off.'

'Now you're being cynical,' he said quietly and drained his coffee. He glanced at his watch. 'I must go. Do I have your promise, Gail?'

She put her head a little on one side. 'To be more selective in my company for the rest of the week?' He nodded. 'No, I don't think so,' she said stubbornly. 'If people want to talk— well, let them! I couldn't care what they say or

123

think about me.'

Tony rose swiftly to his feet, his tall body quivering with swift anger. 'Then care what Blair would think if he heard any of the gossip—believe me, it will reach his ears soon. He doesn't miss much of what goes on here. I'm sure he'll be delighted to hear that his niece has already earned herself a reputation within a week of working at Blair Holiday Camp.'

Gail stared up at him. Her lips quivered briefly. 'I think you do believe I deserve that reputation, Tony,' she said and her voice sounded stunned.

'Think what you like!' he snapped and walked away from her. They had been talking in low tones and had been the subject of many glances and much conjecture while they sat together with their heads close. Tony's last words, spoken sharply, brought wonderment and bewilderment to those who heard him.

'One big happy family!' teased a camper who rose at the same time and almost collided with Tony as he turned angrily away.

'Just rehearsing a sketch for the concert,' Tony improvised quickly and forced a cheerful smile to his lips. 'We never stop working, you know—always on the go here!'

Gail still sat where he left her, but she was oblivious of her surroundings. She had completely forgotten for the moment that Roger waited for her at the tennis courts.

Fierce anger possessed her—anger against the petty minds of those people who could read evil into her association with Roger and his friends—anger against Tony for reminding her forcibly that once she had given her affections impulsively to him—anger, too, that he had tried to enforce any authority he might have over her. She certainly wouldn't hurt Roger by shunning his company for the last two days— he would never understand her motives and, besides, she was too fond of him to want to give up the last days of his holiday with him. It would be painful enough to say goodbye to him on Saturday—no, not goodbye—*au revoir*, they had decided, for Gail knew that Roger was sincere in wanting to see her again and she was determined to go out with him when the season had ended and she was in London for a few weeks. Perhaps he was only nineteen. Age was not always important and Roger was certainly mature enough for an older man. There was no romance in their feeling for each other—they were simply friends and why shouldn't a woman be friendly with a man without the world thinking evil of the association?

At last she got to her feet and left the cafeteria. She found that Tony was just on his way back to find her again. He caught her arm and said in a low voice which nevertheless was very firm: 'If you don't discourage this Roger, then I shall speak to him—and I don't want to do that. I've no wish to embarrass him or humiliate you—but I'm not going to let the camp have a bad name—or you either for that matter.'

Gail looked up into his eyes which were very dark at that moment and she caught her breath at the determination in their depths. She knew that he meant what he said. Without replying, she moved away from him, swinging her tennis racquet, but she knew what she was going to do. She went back to her chalet and changed from her tennis outfit into a simple blue dress. Then she went over to Johnny's chalet and knocked on his door. In answer to his call, she opened the door and entered. He was lying on his bed reading the daily paper.

He thrust it aside. 'Well, this is an honour.'

She went straight to the point. 'Johnny, can I change my mind? Would you take me into Midleigh now—before lunch?'

He rolled off the bed and straightened up. 'Of course.' He looked at her closely. 'What's up, Gail—you look a little grim?'

She shrugged her slim shoulders and smiled briefly. 'Just another argument with Tony.'

He sighed. Taking a comb from his pocket, he tidied his unruly fair hair. 'I wish you two could be friends,' he said ruefully. 'Tony's a grand chap really—I can't understand why you don't get on with each other.'

Gail shrugged again carelessly. 'Natural enemies, I suppose.'

126

He turned round and slipped an arm around her shoulders. 'Natural enemies usually fall in love with each other in the long run if they're opposite sexes,' he said lightly. 'I wouldn't want that to happen. Couldn't you just arrange a friendly truce?' His words brought a laugh to her lips and suddenly her anger left her and she realized how silly it was to argue with Tony when he was possibly only thinking of her anyway. He had impressed upon her that he didn't like gossip when it was linked with her—perhaps after all in his heart he remembered those halcyon days three years ago and carried a tender memory and an unwelcome affection for her.

CHAPTER ELEVEN

Roger came in search of Gail on Saturday morning to say goodbye. She looked up with impulsive welcome in her eyes and, seeing the reproach in his, she knew that she had hurt him badly during the last two days. He had accepted her casual explanation that Thursday had been her free day and she had forgotten their tennis date in her eagerness to get away from the camp for a few hours. He had been a little bewildered, but had made no reproach.

She had volunteered her services for the concert and, although she had no entertainment value, she had made herself useful behind the scenes, making up the artistes, helping to dress the chorus and running here, there and everywhere for Tony who used his skill for organization to the full. He had been particularly nice to Gail, as if sensing her motives for offering her help when she could have been out front with her friends enjoying the concert. Gail had known a second surprise when Johnny had proved to be a clever comedian and mimic. He had not betrayed the fact that he was taking part in the concert, but had merely insisted on being back at the camp early in case he was needed to relieve Tony from irksome duties so he could concentrate on the preparations for the evening.

Friday had been a busy day in the office for they were getting ready for the fresh intake of campers, so she did not take any extra free time during the day. In the evening, at the Carnival Dance, she had studiously avoided spending all her time with Roger, Terry and the others. She had danced once or twice with Roger and been deliberately light-hearted with him, skilfully evading any attempts at serious conversation on his part. Most of the evening she spent circulating among the other campers and helping Johnny to organize the novelty dances. At the end of the dance she had slipped away before Roger could invite her to swim with him and the others.

Now she smiled at him. 'Now I know why everyone hates Saturdays,' she said. 'It's terribly depressing to say goodbyes.'

'It is for me,' he said in low tones. He threw himself into the basket chair beside her. 'This has been the best holiday of my life,' he said abruptly.

'I'm glad,' she said sincerely.

'You've made it so,' he said and there was the ring of truth in his voice. 'You know I've fallen in love with you, don't you, Gail?' Startled, she did not know what to say. The colour flooded her cheeks and it was impossible to look away from his compelling eyes. 'Of course you know,' he went on. 'That's why you've been avoiding me these last two

days. I'm not a fool. I know that's the reason—
I know too that you don't give a damn for
me . . .'

'That's not true!' Gail protested swiftly. 'I'm
very fond of you, Roger. We've had a lot of fun
this week and I'm glad we met.'

He leaned forward eagerly, heartened by
her words. 'Will you write to me, Gail? You
did promise—but I thought you might have
changed your mind. And will you still meet me
in London at the end of the season and come
to a concert with me?'

Gail nodded. 'Of course I will.' She laid her
hand on his arm. 'I'm sorry you've got too
deeply involved, Roger,' she said quietly. 'But I
think it's easy to grow fond of someone in a
place like this. The atmosphere is so conducive
to it. I think that when you get home again and
see things in their proper perspective, you'll
realize that you're simply fond of me and
certainly not in love with me. I hope so,
anyway.'

'I know I'm younger than you,' he said,
looking down at the cigarette he turned
between his long, slender fingers. 'But it hasn't
seemed to matter—I don't think it ever would.
I shall always love you, Gail—and I shall look
forward to your letters and to seeing you at the
end of the summer.' He looked up quickly.
'You won't let me down?' Gail shook her head.
'Is there anyone else?' he asked shyly,
betraying his youth by the hesitancy of the

question. 'If there wasn't, I'd go on hoping that one day . . .' He broke off and searched her eyes eagerly.

When he had finally gone with one last look back, Gail knew that she had done the right thing. It had been difficult to emphasize that he didn't stand a chance of winning her love without hurting him, but she knew that she would never think of Roger in that light. Not while she loved Tony, anyway, and she knew her feelings would never alter. Thinking of Tony, she realized that he had been in exactly the same predicament as herself, three years ago, and now she could understand why he had been deliberately offhand and cruel. He had done the kindest thing in his eyes: she was young and infatuated and had made her interest as obvious as Roger had done where she was concerned. She hoped that soon Roger would recover not from the effects of their friendship which she felt could continue for many years—but from the love which burned in his youthful heart and made life seem empty at present because it was not returned.

She was sorry to see the crowd of young people go, because it had been a very happy week and she had found them both entertaining and lively. The camp seemed empty without them, although several campers remained for another week and some new ones had already arrived. One could tell the new arrivals by their expressions which indicated a slight fear that the camp would not live up to expectations, a hesitancy in entering any of the buildings, and eagerness to find out all about the place which was to be their home for one brief week in the year.

Tony crossed the ballroom from his office and his eyes narrowed a little as he caught sight of Gail, sitting in one of the comfortable basket chairs, rather a forlorn figure. He paused by her chair, his hand resting on the back of it. 'I see your young friends have gone,' he said casually.

'I hope you noticed that I took your advice,' she returned coolly, turning to look up at him. 'It wasn't very pleasant for me to hurt that nice boy.'

'You showed common sense,' he approved. 'One sometimes has to be cruel to be kind, Gail.'

Words flashed into her brain and she opened her lips to retort that she knew very well how he dealt with similar situations. Then she pulled herself up sharply. If Tony ever discovered that she had loved him three years ago with real depth of emotion and that her love was still strong in her being, life would become impossible for them both. So she merely said: 'It does happen that love is mistaken for infatuation in some cases.'

'And infatuation is frequently mistaken for love—especially by young people,' Tony returned smoothly.

'I think Roger really is sincere in his affection for me,' Gail said mulishly.

He smiled. 'But you're consoling yourself with the thought that Roger will forget all about the pangs of love within a few days. Out of sight and out of mind, you know! As for you, Gail—this time next week you'll be just as miserable because another young man who fancied you to be the answer to his prayers has gone home suffering from unrequited love.'

'How unpleasant you are!' she snapped. 'I won't make the same mistakes again, anyway. In future, I'll steer clear of entanglements with the campers—then no one can be hurt and no one can talk about me.'

Tony laughed. She was so delightfully young. 'My dear Gail, you're too attractive to be overlooked. If it isn't the campers, it will be the staff—I'm afraid romance runs rife in these places. You'll have similar trouble with several young men throughout the season, if I'm any judge of human nature.'

She ignored the compliment. 'Well, it's never likely to arise with you,' she told him angrily.

'I hope not.' He was suddenly very serious. 'I'd hate to hurt you again, Gail.'

'You're impossible!' she threw at him. 'You know very well that I meant the boot to be on the other foot!'

He smiled and, without answering, walked

away, leaving Gail to fume. She did not fume for long. Her sense of humour came to the fore and a laugh bubbled to her lips as she made her way back to Reception after her break.

Just before lunch, Howard entered the Reception Block. He waited until Gail was free for a moment and then he went over to the desk. 'Come and have lunch with me, Gail, when you can get away,' he invited. 'I've seen hardly anything of you this week.'

'Thanks, Howard—I'd love to,' she enthused. She smiled warmly at her uncle and then turned to a fresh batch of campers with the same rich smile still touching her lips. It was an enchanting welcome for any weary traveller and several brightened perceptibly. Howard nodded to himself as he watched her coping efficiently with the intake and then he slipped away.

Ann overheard the brief exchange and she turned to Tony where he stood at the big glass doors welcoming the newcomers. 'Gail's honoured,' she said lightly. 'Howard seems to have taken a fancy to her—although I would have said that Clare was more his type.'

'Jealous?' teased Tony. Knowing the relationship between Blair and Gail, he saw nothing odd in the invitation to lunch. It was difficult to remember that he, Johnny and Clare were the only ones who were in the know.

Ann raised a supercilious eyebrow. 'I haven't the slightest interest in the boss,' she said coolly. 'But one can hardly say the same for his secretary.'

'Why are you so hard on Gail? I thought you were quite good friends.' There was a reproof in his tone and Ann's eyes were suddenly repentent as she glanced up at him.

'I'm sorry,' she said. 'It wasn't a very nice thing to say—I wasn't insinuating anything beastly really. But it does seem rather unexpected for Howard to take an interest in any of the staff out of business hours.'

'Susan used to lunch with Blair very often,' Tony reminded her. 'It's just an excuse to talk business—Blair's one and only interest.'

'Gail's far more attractive than Susan—and a much sweeter person. I wouldn't blame any man for taking an interest in her.' Inwardly, she supposed one could hardly blame Tony for taking up the cudgels in Gail's defence, although that had been surprising. He treated Gail very casually: at times there almost seemed to be an enmity between them which disturbed Ann. Yet that strange thing called intuition led Ann to believe that something existed between Tony and Gail which neither of them wanted to admit. Suddenly Ann exclaimed. 'Oh Lor! Here comes another coach load!' She followed Tony out of the Reception Block to greet the campers and for the moment Gail was forgotten.

135

It was odd but true that Howard had seen little of Gail during the previous week. The first week of the season was always a busy one and he liked to wander about the camp, keeping an ear open for complaints, noting what the campers approved or didn't approve, making sure that nothing had been forgotten on the organization, entertainment or welfare side, and watchful of any intrigues between staff and campers. The latter were not unusual and Howard took steps to cut them short. He would take the guilty member of the staff to one side and with a few sharp words warn him or her that if it occurred too frequently it would mean the loss of his or her job. Maybe it was harsh, but it was his point of view that the young people came to the camp on holiday and in search of romance, whether they realized it or not. If one of the staff concentrated on a pretty girl, it prevented a camper from finding a possible partner in life—if a male camper preferred the company of a waitress, then there was always the possibility that a girl on holiday would remain a wallflower all week. Very little escaped Howard Blair's notice, for he had a keen eye, keen hearing and an unfailing instinct for the wrong note in any relationship. He knew every member of his staff by name and appearance and it owed much to his concern for their welfare, as equally as the campers, that Blair was a very happy camp with few jarring situations throughout the season.

He knew of Gail's friendship with the crowd of young men and girls. The staff might assume that he turned a blind eye to the activities of Gail Anson but this was not true, and he had another motive for inviting his niece to lunch, apart from wanting the pleasure of her company. He was very fond of her and his affection had grown stronger during the past weeks. He knew of the talk among the staff and disliked it. Knowing Gail so well, he felt sure that the talk was malicious and untrue, but nevertheless he was determined to prevent any further such talk in the coming weeks.

They had finished their lunch before he broached the subject. Sitting in the cool lounge and mourning the rain which fell heavily outside, he lit a cigarette for her and then said quietly: 'I'm glad to see that you're quite happy with us, Gail.'

She smiled at him, her face radiant. 'It's all such fun, Howard.'

He returned her smile. 'I hope you'll still think so when the novelty wears off, my dear.' He looked momentarily anxious. 'I'm not working you too hard, I hope. You look a little pale today.'

She turned an affectionate but reproachful gaze on him, and said quickly: 'Working too hard! When I've spent more time with the campers than in the office all week! I think you're exceptionally kind and considerate.'

He noted those words: 'with the campers', and decided this was his opportunity. 'I've seen you with the campers several times, Gail. One particular group of youngsters, mostly. Nice crowd, weren't they?'

'Very nice!' she enthused. Her face clouded a little. 'But I hated to say goodbye to them all.'

He nodded. 'That's one of the drawbacks here,' he said. 'It doesn't pay to get attached to anyone—one must always remember that they're here for a very short time and then they go out of one's life for ever.' He paused, not wishing to hurt her. 'You won't take it amiss if I suggest that in future you avoid spending too much time with any particular person or group, Gail?'

The quick veiling of her lovely eyes told him that she had been expecting his words. He wondered if reproach or annoyance or pain reflected in their depths.

'I've already decided to share myself equally among them all in future,' she said quietly. Had Tony been telling tales, after all? Or had Howard simply heard some of the gossip for himself?

'Sensible girl,' he approved. 'Look, Gail, as far as I'm concerned, you're a free agent. It's none of my business how you spend your free time—or who you're with. But you know the rules which apply to my staff—and to all intents and purposes, you're one of my staff and must abide by those rules. It's a difficult position, as you realize. Of course, I could let it be known that you're my niece and then you wouldn't be criticized . . .'

'Of course I would,' Gail broke in firmly. 'Even more so, in fact. The others would resent me and imply that I was favoured. I don't want that, Howard. I'd much rather let them think that I'm an ordinary paid member of your staff—as for the rules, Tony has already pointed them out to me with a few riders of his own,' she added bitterly.

A flicker of interest sparked in Howard's eyes. With his keen perception, he had noticed that Gail and Tony strangely did not hit it off. There seemed to be no apparent reason for this. Even more disturbing was a feeling that beneath the animosity was an intimate knowledge of each other which surely was not possible—unless they had known each other before and Gail would have mentioned it to him, Howard was convinced. He had difficulty in actually putting his finger on any definite reason for their dislike of each other. He disregarded the age-old idea that mutual dislike came unbidden and unexpected. In his experience, there was usually a motive: fear, distrust, jealousy or unrecognized affection. For his money, Howard took the last named. It would please him very much to see Gail and Tony make a match of it—but remembering

139

Tony's light and somewhat flirtatious approach to women in the past, he doubted if that young man was capable of anything deeper. Gail was the more likely person to fall in love with real intensity—but there was no evidence to indicate that Tony Sheppard was the type of man she would choose for the recipient of her heart. Since she had come to Blair, her attentions had been mainly centred on Johnny—who was even less capable of sustaining an interest in any woman, in Howard Blair's opinion. Young, personable men who worked in holiday camps had a great many opportunities for flirtation and both Tony and Johnny had used their opportunities to the full in the past. It was harmless enough and a sign of their youth, and provided it was recognized as mere flirtation on both sides, Howard had no objection. So far, neither of them had made his attentions the subject of gossip and they both avoided seeking out any one woman among the campers so obviously that she was bowled over by their looks, personality and charm. When that happened—if it did—then Howard would step in quickly. It would be rather ironic, he told himself now, if that woman turned out to be his own niece, young, vulnerable and attractive Gail with her inborn innocence and instinctive trust.

'You mustn't take exception to Tony's manner,' he said now soothingly. 'I expect he understands that you've been a little swept off your feet this week by a host of young people who obviously enjoyed and wanted your company. He's trying to prevent you from being hurt—and you know, Gail, my dear, that could happen week after week if you give your affections too lightly and impulsively.'

'Oh, I keep a tight rein on my affections these days,' Gail returned, but there was a swift pain in her breast, like a knife turning, as she recalled the days when they had run wild, only to bring her humiliation and tears. 'I learnt long ago that it doesn't pay to show anyone that you're fond of them—least of all men!' There was definite bitterness in her tone now and Howard looked at her sharply, thinking she was too young to speak of men in such a way and wondering who had hurt her to such an extent that the memory of pain still lingered.

CHAPTER TWELVE

Gail paused at the top of the steps which led up to the swimming-pool and looked about her, unaware of the attractive figure she made in her swimsuit or the many eyes that turned admiringly towards her. The wooden seats that were spaced about the pool were all occupied: many recumbent figures sunbathed on the grass surround; happy holiday-makers swam and dived and frolicked in the clear blue water. It was Sunday afternoon and Gail's free time. She meant to take full advantage of the sunshine which bathed their quiet corner of England.

A man ran up the steps and paused too. 'Ready for the Beauty Contest?' he asked her lightly. 'I'll put my money on you, I think, despite the competition.'

Gail smiled at him. She had already grown used to the easy familiarity of the campers and learnt to take such remarks at their superficial value. 'I'm not entering,' she replied.

'Of course you are,' he said, surprised. 'You're not shy, are you? My mates and I will see that you go in for it.' He grinned.

'I'm afraid I'm not eligible—I'm on the staff,' Gail explained quickly.

He accepted her explanation with a nod. 'Oh well, it gives the other girls a chance,' he told her. He eyed her approvingly. 'Swimming or sunbathing?'

'Both—but the pool is very crowded.'

'What do you expect on a day like this?' He indicated the sun high overhead, the cloudless blue sky, the heat haze over the sea. 'Joining some friends?' he asked the next moment. 'Why don't you come and sunbathe with me and my mates?' he invited. 'We've got a portable radio—and they're quite good fun.'

Gail shook her head. 'Thanks—but I can see some of my friends. I think I'll join them.' It wasn't true, but she made a point of discouraging any camper who sought more than passing familiarity these days.

'Okay.' He was not perturbed. There were plenty of girls in the camp. 'Perhaps I'll see you in the ballroom tonight—I'll look out for you. Do you like dancing?' When she nodded, he added, 'Okay. Reserve me a couple.' Then he went on his way, around the pool, down the steps the other side and crossed the grass lawn to a group of campers.

Gail walked along the edge of the pool. She came to a seat that was only half full. She threw her towel on to the vacant part, slipped off her sandals and then turned to smile at the campers who spoke to her. They were joined by a young man who climbed out of the pool and came over to the seat, water dripping from his lithe body, which was deeply tanned. His fair hair was bleached by the sun and his eyes were strikingly blue in his sunburnt face. He picked up Gail's towel and began to rub his chest.

'That isn't your towel, Ted,' a woman told him quickly.

He looked down at it. Then he turned rueful eyes on Gail who watched him with a smile just touching her lips. 'Sorry,' he said with a grin. 'I didn't even look at it.'

'That's all right,' she told him. She glanced at his brown body. 'You look as if you've had a holiday already this year,' she said lightly.

'I've just come back from abroad,' he said. 'It's a sight hotter over there than England. Going in?' he added, with a jerk of his head towards the pool.

It struck Gail again, as it so often did, that these young men on holiday were very obvious in their approach. It was apparent that she meant to enter the pool, for she was fastening her bathing cap as he spoke. But she merely replied, 'Yes. It's very inviting—what's the water like?'

'Cold.' And he shivered slightly. 'At least, it seems cold after swimming in the Mediterranean.' He grinned again. Gail approved his nice open smile, white teeth flashing in his bronzed face and reflecting in the pleasant blue eyes. 'Are you a good swimmer?' he asked.

Gail shrugged. 'I get by. I can do the length if I make an effort.'

He laughed. 'Pity—I hoped I'd have the job of saving your life.'

Gail read the open admiration in his eyes, but she merely stepped to the water's edge and surveyed the pool. The young man came to stand beside her. 'How would you like to be thrown in?' he asked teasingly.

She smiled up at him. 'No, thanks.' Then she executed a neat shallow dive and felt the water close over her head. When she surfaced, she turned on to her back and found the young man called Ted close beside her. 'It is cold,' she told him accusingly.

'Well, I warned you,' he replied with a grin.

Gail swam to the side and caught the bar. There was scarcely room to swim without being either bumped or splashed. It was better at night when few campers were hardy enough to enter the pool. She reminded herself that they paid for the privilege of using the pool and she had no right to complain if it were crowded by day.

The young man was close beside her again. 'You're not getting out already?' he asked and he sounded a little disappointed. 'It isn't too cold for you, surely.'

'I'm having a breather and assessing my chances of getting to the other side without being drowned by some enthusiastic swimmer,' she retorted.

Ted laughed. 'Awful, isn't it? I think I'll keep my swimming for midnight in future—

then I'll have the pool to myself.'

Gail smiled. 'That's what you think,' she told him lightly. 'A lot of the staff use the pool at night and so do quite a few campers who don't like crowds.' She shot away from him suddenly in a fast crawl, her feet moving rhythmically, her style both clean and swift. Once or twice she had to veer direction to avoid other swimmers. She turned swiftly, neatly on the other side of the pool and swam back again. She found Ted's eyes on her, admiring, approving and perhaps a little envious.

'With a style like that, you should win all the events in the Gala on Thursday,' he told her.

'I'm not allowed to enter,' Gail said. 'I'm on the staff.'

'That explains it,' he said cryptically. 'So far, all the pretty girls I've seen work for the camp,' he added in explanation. 'It doesn't seem fair.'

Gail laughed and climbed out of the pool. She pulled off her bathing cap and shook out her short dark curls which were slightly damp. Quickly she rubbed her body with her towel. She felt refreshed, exhilarated and a little breathless from her exertions. Without stopping to speak again to Ted, she gathered up her things and went down the steps. Entering the cafeteria, she bought a cup of tea and sat down at one of the tables. A few minutes later, Tony came into the cafeteria. He glanced in her direction and she acknowledged him with a brief smile. She was a little surprised when he joined her a few seconds afterwards with a steaming cup of tea.

'Caught in the rain?' he asked drily, indicating her still-wet swimsuit and damp curls.

Gail laughed lightly. Suddenly her heart was singing because Tony had sought her out of his own volition and he seemed to be in a friendly mood. Quite unthinkingly, she asked: 'Where's Johnny—I haven't seen him for hours.'

'Johnny? Oh, he's around.' Tony indicated the camp vaguely. 'Why? Are you waiting for him?'

'Oh no!' she disclaimed quickly, too quickly it seemed to Tony, who glanced at her flushed face and wondered if she was more than just fond of Johnny.

Tony brought out cigarettes. Glancing at his nicotine-stained fingers, Gail thought briefly that he smoked too much and then reminded herself that his was a hectic life and perhaps cigarettes were his only relaxation. He said abruptly: 'When the Beauty Contest is over, I'm free for a couple of hours. It's your afternoon off, too, isn't it?'

'Yes,' replied Gail, wondering what was coming.

'Do you want to come for a drive along the coast?' he asked.

Because the invitation surprised her, Gail said lightly: 'This is so sudden!' When he scowled a little, she added swiftly, 'I've never known you want to get away from the camp— even for a couple of hours, Tony. Don't you feel well?' Her tone was mocking.

He picked up a spoon and stirred his tea. 'I am human, you know, despite the common rumour in the camp.' He spoke sharply. 'Coming or not?' he added and his tone inferred that he was indifferent to her acceptance or otherwise.

Resenting his tone, it was on the tip of Gail's tongue to refuse curtly. Then she looked at his profile and saw that it was downcast. She said quietly: 'Thanks, Tony. I'd like to come with you.'

He turned his head and looked at her. A slow smile broke across his face and he was totally unaware that her heart turned over in her breast. 'I'll look out for you just after four, then.'

She nodded. 'I must change into something dry,' she said and rose awkwardly, disturbed by his nearness. He did not answer and as she turned to go, two girl campers came over to his table and sat down with Tony, greeting him familiarly and lightly. He answered them, smiling in the slow way that immediately attracted all women, and Gail left him indulging in the mild flirtation that seemed to come so naturally to him. The feeling that flooded through her she recognized as jealousy and chided herself for her own stupidity. It was part of Tony's job to be pleasant to the girls who flocked to his side wherever he went, eager to attract the handsome organizer and anxious to impress their friends with their success. But Tony was the same to every girl—charming, quick with his easy flattery, and attentive. Bitterly, Gail told herself it was part of his showmanship and he had only given her the same easy attentions in order to ensure that his attractions hadn't faded before the season started. It might be three years ago, but it was as clear as yesterday to Gail and she knew that forgive him she might, but never forget that she had given him her impulsive heart to meet with amusement and perhaps contempt.

As she stripped off her wet swimsuit and rubbed her slim body dry, Gail wondered again why he had invited her to share his few precious hours of free time. She did not delude herself that he was attracted to her. Johnny had told her many times that it was relaxation for him to be with her because she was undemanding company and a good listener. Perhaps Tony too sensed this in her. He was surely in need of relaxation, for while he was on duty he could never lower his guard and completely be himself. But during the few hours that afternoon, he might once again be the man she had known three years ago, gay, charming without effort, and very appealing. Gail knew that she must never, by word or gesture, betray that she was still in love with Tony, and as she dressed in a cool linen frock she mentally girded her loins for the ordeal of being with him alone and away from the watchful eyes of staff and campers and tempted to show in some way that her feelings had not changed despite the years between.

Tony was a good driver, competent and confident. But whereas Johnny chattered away easily while he drove, Tony was silent and Gail wondered if he were concentrating on the road or was merely glad that for once there was no necessity for idle conversation.

They drove along the coast road for some miles, then Tony pulled in at a small bay. The tide was out and the sands stretched golden before them. In the distance, the sea was calm and serene. It was a secluded little bay and Tony and Gail were the only invaders of the quiet peace.

Tony stripped off his shirt and lay flat on his back on the sand. His body was powerful, lithe and tanned. He closed his eyes and let the sun ease out the tiredness and strain. Gail sat near him on the sand, her knees drawn up and her hands clasped about them. While he lay with closed eyes, she could study him openly and adoration was in her expression for his manly good looks, the lean curve of his cheek, the straight, slender nose, the length of dark lashes and the purposeful strength of mouth and chin. She longed to trace the attractive profile with her finger but dared not. The urge to lean forward and kiss the mobile lips grew stronger and she forced herself to look away, out to sea, to think of other than the sweet desire which ran through her entire being. This love for a man who was deliberately cold to her was intolerable but unquenchable, and sadness was in her heart.

She was startled when he spoke, turning her head towards him with the swift movement and grace of a startled bird. 'I'm afraid I'm not very good company. You must be bored.'

'No, no, I'm not,' she assured him. 'It's so lovely here.'

'It's very peaceful,' he acknowledged. 'I usually come here by myself whenever I get the chance. Much as I love the camp and the campers, sometimes I long to be alone and have done with the constant activity and demands.' His eyes were open now and centred on her small face. 'I asked you to come with me on an impulse. Afterwards, I thought I'd regret it, for you're usually a talkative little soul. But you've been surprisingly quiet and understanding, Gail.'

She smiled at him. 'Everyone has a different side to his nature, Tony.'

He nodded. 'True. Most people are very complex, I've found. No one is as easy to read as it seems on the surface.'

Gail laughed lightly. 'That's why people are so interesting.'

Something flickered in his eyes for a moment. 'I'm beginning to think it's time I revised my opinion of you.'

The slightest trace of a flush stained her cheeks. She looked away from him. 'If it's a bad opinion, of course you should.'

'Neither good nor bad,' he offered. 'Mostly indifferent.'

Her eyes flashed. 'That's only too obvious.'

He caught her hand and held it tightly. 'We didn't come here to quarrel, Gail. Let's keep that for the camp.' He smiled disarmingly. She tried to free her hand, but he merely laughed at her with his eyes and tightened his grip. Suddenly he jerked and, taken off balance, she fell across him. His chest was hard and masculine beneath her soft body. He was smiling into her eyes and there was something akin to triumph in their depths. His other arm went around her and held her close to him. A momentary fear disturbed her and she struggled to loosen his hold. His eyes narrowed sleepily. 'How long is it since I kissed you?' he asked softly. She did not reply but strained to avoid his eyes. 'Apparently too long,' he said and the next moment he moved swiftly so that she was lying on the sand with his arms about her and his lips on hers. She had forgotten the wonder of his kisses. He was very experienced and within seconds she gave up the struggle and surrendered to the flame of love which surged through her veins.

Tony was bewildered and startled by the intensity of her response and when their lips finally parted, he lay very still, not attempting to kiss her again, his arms still about her but without pressure in their hold. To him the kiss had meant nothing. He kissed many women and knew the familiar surge of triumph when they accepted his kisses without demur. But this time there was no triumph. He felt a little ashamed of himself—and this was a new emotion for Tony Sheppard. When he brought Gail to this secluded spot, there had been no intention in his mind of kissing her. But she had been appealing and lovely with her cheeks glowing, the dark hair a little windswept from the open car, eyes shining as she looked at him and then looked away as though afraid of what he might read in them. Desire had flickered and he had obeyed the urge to know the sweetness of her lips. But he had not expected the intensity of ardour from her or the willingness which she betrayed to give more than her lips to him. The knowledge that he could easily have possessed her completely had effectually killed all desire in him.

Gail wondered at his stillness. She knew that she had responded too ardently and she dreaded a repeat of that awful time three years ago when he had made it very clear that his kisses were casual and without depth. Her heart ached and the tears were very near the surface. Her hand was about his shoulders and she squeezed gently, to waken him from the trance into which he had apparently fallen. He turned his head and looked at her. His eyes were guarded and she knew swift disappointment. 'What's the matter, Tony?' she whispered haltingly.

He released himself and sat up abruptly. 'Nothing. I suppose we should make a move. We'll find somewhere to have a cup of tea before we go back to the camp.'

The casualness of his words smote her and she realized again that her love was futile. Without a word, she sat up and smoothed her dress, searched for a comb in her handbag and sleeked back the dark curls. The tension between them was very pronounced and Gail regretted that she had accepted his invitation in the first place. It had been more than heavenly to know his arms about her again and his lips on hers but the realization that his kisses had been casual flirtation opened up the old pain in her heart.

Tony rose to his feet and brushed the sand from his grey slacks. Then he bent down, picked up his shirt and slipped it on, buttoning it, looking out over the sands to the sea. If Gail was still in love with him, then he had been cruel to bring her here, to make love to her. But he argued that it was gossip among the staff that Gail gave her kisses lightly even though they might seem ardent. She might be merely a good actress. How little he really knew her—and it was his own fault because he had not tried to discover the real Gail. Perhaps she was nothing but a tramp, really. It was true enough that she responded to the light familiarity of the campers. He had seen her dancing close to men on the ballroom floor and she made no secret of the fact that she enjoyed male company. A few moments ago she would have given herself to him willingly—perhaps he was not the only one to whom she would extend her favours.

It did not occur to him that behind all these ugly thoughts lurked disappointment, for he had believed implicitly in Gail's innocence and defended her against all the rumours. He misinterpreted her willing surrender to his kisses and so he was disappointed in her.

CHAPTER THIRTEEN

The only thing which comforted Gail was the thought that if Tony had kissed her casually, then perhaps he kissed Ann as casually. She had not been able to forget the night when Ann did not come in until half-past two and Tony had kissed her outside the chalet door. She had made no mention of it to Ann but that chatterbox had frequently spoken of Tony and how much she liked him, how different he really was when away from the camp and the campers. Gail had endeavoured to hide the jealousy which burned within her and Ann was too shallow a person to sense it in her chalet mate. They were quite good friends, although their busy lives prevented them from being together very much. Ann was a popular member of the staff and her evenings were always sprinkled with dates—some with the staff and some with campers, for she was very contemptuous of rules and regulations. But she was very discreet too and seldom caused gossip in the camp. Gail sometimes wondered bitterly why it was that if ever she encouraged attention from one of the campers, it was invariably all over the camp within a few hours, yet Ann's actions never invited comment.

Relations between Gail and Tony were

strained on the way back to the camp. Even when they pulled up for tea at a small café, Tony's conversation had centred on the camp and its activities as though he feared to bring any personal subject into life. Gail was unhappy and subdued and relieved when they finally reached the camp and Tony dropped her off at the Reception Block before he drove on to garage his sports car. She thanked him for the outing. He merely nodded briefly and drove on. Gail looked after him and it was an effort to fight down the tears which stung her eyelids and brought an ache to her throat. But pride came to the rescue and she walked to her chalet with her head high and a determination burning in her breast that never again would she give Tony the opportunity to humiliate her with his casual kisses.

That same evening in the ballroom the young man whom she knew as Ted sought her out, making no secret of his admiration and liking. Defiantly, she encouraged him, telling herself that she didn't care if people talked about her and unhappy enough to think that she might just as well give them something definite as food for gossip. She was lively and gay, talkative, easily amused by Ted's simple humour, indifferent to the furore she caused among the campers by her wild behaviour. She spent the entire evening with Ted. She danced with him, allowing him to hold her close and press his head against her hair, made no protest to the murmured endearments, the light kisses he bestowed on her hair and cheek. When he asked her to go with him into the fresh air for a few minutes, she agreed, uncaring for the many eyes that watched their progress down the length of the ballroom and through the glass doors. They wandered hand in hand up to the swimming-pool and watched the young boys in the water. Then they crossed the lawns and playing fields and went down to the beach. Ted amused himself by picking up pebbles and throwing them into the sea. He was young and attractive and entertaining. He was good-looking too and Gail liked him. But she did not expect him to turn suddenly towards her and pull her into his arms. His lips were hot and demanding on hers and his hands urgent and restless. Gail struggled and protested, but his blood was on fire and the beach was deserted. His kisses became more and more ardent and Gail trembled in his arms, afraid of his strength and passion. She stopped fighting him, thinking with craft born of fear that if he thought her willing she could the more easily elude him with a sudden movement.

It was just as she melted against his tall, powerful body and his arms tightened about her that Tony reached the stone wall which ran along the top of the beach. His eyes were suddenly hard and his mouth took on a grim line. Without further thought, he leaped down on to the sand and strode forward. Ted heard the crunch of sand underfoot and raised his head. The relaxation of his grip gave Gail her opportunity. She slipped from his arms and then saw Tony. Her eyes filled with relief and gratitude for his opportune arrival. But Tony barely glanced at her. He did not dare to interfere in a camper's private affairs, but he found it difficult not to show his anger and violent disillusionment. Gail quailed at the expression in his eyes. Surely he did not think that she had welcomed Ted's advances? But it was apparent from his face that he did, and she knew that she had finally convinced him that his bad opinion of her was justified.

Tony forced a smile as he reached them. 'Sorry to interrupt, old man, but I'm looking for Gail.' He turned to her and his tone was icy. 'Johnny wants you in the ballroom.'

'Okay, Tony. I'll be there in a minute.' She did not intend to hurry back as though he had cracked a whip, much as she longed to get away from the amorous Ted whose kisses had been so unexpected and certainly unwanted.

'He's waiting for you,' came Tony's sharp reply.

She smiled lightly at Ted. 'Always in demand, you see! Coming back?'

His passion had cooled instantly when Tony came on the scene but he was a little annoyed at the untimely interruption. 'We came out for some fresh air,' he said stiffly to Tony as they

159

began to walk back in the direction of the camp.

Tony nodded. 'It gets very stuffy in the ballroom,' he said lightly.

'What does Johnny want me for?' Gail asked coldly.

'I didn't ask him,' Tony replied shortly. It had been a fabrication of the moment and surely Gail was quick enough on the uptake to realize that.

As they entered the ballroom, Ted said, 'Well, I'll go back to my crowd, Gail. Don't forget to join us when you're through with Johnny.'

'See you around,' she replied automatically as he strode across the big room. As soon as he was out of hearing, she turned to Tony. 'Thank goodness you turned up,' she said warmly. 'He was getting difficult to handle.'

'That's rather surprising when one considers your experience with men,' he retorted coldly.

The colour drained from her face. 'Then you think I encouraged him?' she demanded angrily.

'I know you did,' he said. 'It's none of my business, of course, but you seemed to be enjoying yourself.'

'Judging by appearances again?' she sneered. 'How little you know about women!'

'I know plenty about you,' he said and now his own temper was rising quickly. 'I might add that I don't like any of it. All I can say is that you certainly live up to the reputation you've earned!'

In the silence caused by the ending of the dance tune his words rang out sharply. Campers stopped talking and turned their eyes in their direction. Gail's hand came up instinctively and she caught him a sound blow on the cheek. There was a gasp of horror which ran around the ballroom. Tony looked down at Gail for one long moment and then he turned on his heel and walked over to his office. The door slammed behind him. Paul raised his baton quickly and the band swung into a noisy quickstep. Gail looked about her, met a battery of accusing eyes and swiftly walked out of the ballroom. The assault was discussed for a few minutes by the staff and campers alike and then they went back to their former conversations and amusements.

Tony stood for a moment in the quiet office, seething with rage, his cheek smarting from the blow. It was not the first time he had been slapped, but never before in public and he felt the humiliation deeply. Despite himself, he admired Gail's spirit, for his words had been cutting, no matter how true. On an impulse, sensing that Gail would have left the ballroom, he opened the door that led from the office out of the building and slipped out. All the angry words which he had longed to throw at Gail but could not because of the interest aroused by the little scene still burned in his brain. He caught sight of Gail's small figure huddled on one of the wooden seats which stood around the swimming-pool. She looked dejected and he wondered if she were in tears. He knew his anger would not withstand the sight of Gail in tears, yet he walked on and up the steps and approached her.

Gail was not crying. She was staring into the water, her eyes on the reflection of the bright lights which floodlighted the swimming-pool but she was unaware of its beauty. She deeply regretted the blow she had dealt Tony, yet she could not find the necessary courage to seek him out to apologize. For it would take courage to face him now, to meet the dark coldness of his eyes, and to stumble over the few words of apology which she felt sure he would grudgingly accept.

She did not hear his approach. But she sensed his presence and looked up. He sat down on the seat next to her. Taking a cigarette from the packet he brought out, he struck a match with fingers that trembled slightly.

'Can I have a cigarette?' Gail asked in a low voice. Without a word, he offered her the packet and she bent her head over the match he held. She murmured her thanks. She inhaled deeply on the cigarette, grateful for its relaxing effect, knowing that all her anger against him had faded and she was only filled with sorrow that she had deliberately struck the man she loved.

He still did not speak and the tension was intolerable. Gail longed to break the silence but the right words would not come and she feared to make matters worse.

At last he said slowly: 'I shall see Blair in the morning and give him my resignation.'

His words startled her. 'But why?'

He threw her a contemptuous glance. 'I should think it must be obvious.'

'Because I slapped you? It will be forgotten by the morning,' she assured him tremulously. 'Anyway, I shall be the one they talk about. I shall be the one who takes all the blame.'

'I'm not only thinking of the campers and what they will say,' he said. He looked down at the cigarette, twisting it in his fingers, watching the grey smoke writhe into the air. 'It's impossible for us to stay in this camp together. Blair will never let you leave—he dotes on you too much. So it means that I'm going.'

'Howard won't accept your resignation,' she said quickly. 'You're invaluable to the camp— it would be nothing without you. There's no need for you to leave. I'll keep out of your way in future.' Her lower lip trembled and she caught it fiercely between her teeth.

He laughed shortly but there was no humour in the sound. 'The camp isn't that big,' he reminded her. He dropped his cigarette and stepped on it, extinguishing the bright glow.

'Tony, I wish we could be friends,' Gail said

abruptly, impulsively. The wish was true enough. What it cost her to put it into words, Tony would never know.

'We're natural enemies,' he replied curtly.

His remark brought back to her something that Johnny had once said on the subject and she was glad that Tony did not see the colour that flooded her small face. But he was not looking at her. Leaning forward, his hands clasped in front of him, he was staring across the pool at the lines of brick-built chalets.

'That isn't true!' she objected. 'We were good friends once. I didn't know you worked here when I wrote to Howard and asked him for a job. I was pleased when I saw you. I couldn't understand why you didn't acknowledge our former friendship. I still don't understand. Neither do I know why you've always been so cold and unfriendly to me since I came to the camp.'

Something snapped inside him and he turned on her fiercely. 'Because it takes very little encouragement for you to think a man is madly in love with you—or for you to imagine yourself in love with him. You chased me blatantly three years ago. I had to tell you then that I wasn't interested—I warned you again when you came here and I'm telling you once more and for the last time. You simply aren't my type!' he threw at her cruelly.

'Then why did you kiss me this morning?' The pain which swept over her felt like death.

She prayed that it would fade as quickly as it had come, yet it lingered for what seemed an eternity.

He gestured contemptuously with his hand. 'A kiss! You're just the sort of girl who thinks a kiss from a man denotes wedding bells! I kiss a great many women and think nothing of it.'

She was very pale and seemed to have grown smaller as she sat beside him, tense and hurt. But she said as though the realization had just come to her: 'Poor Tony! You just don't know what to think about me, do you? In one breath you accuse me of kissing any man who comes along merely because I take that sort of thing lightly. Then in the next breath you tell me that one kiss and I'm thinking of marriage. Do you really think that I'm hoping to marry every man who kisses me? As for that fellow tonight—I didn't want him to kiss me and I would have slapped his face at the first opportunity if you hadn't come along and saved me from his unwelcome advances.'

'How dramatic!' he sneered. 'Sir Galahad— that's me, I suppose. And the lady in distress falls at my feet in gratitude and offers me her all?' But in his heart he admitted that she was right: he didn't know what to believe of her and he resented the confusion of his thoughts and emotions; it would be simple if he could define her as one particular type and lose interest in her. It was because there seemed so many sides to her character that he had bothered to defend her from the gossip and believe in her innocence. He suddenly realized that he had been concerned for her all the time since she had come to the camp; but he brushed the thought aside, telling himself it was only because they had known each other before that interest had flickered.

They were silent for a moment. Then Gail asked with pain in her voice: 'So you think I've been chasing you, Tony?'

He shrugged. 'Not obviously—but most women are subtle. I think you'd be thrilled if I paid you any attention. You made no protest when I kissed you today—in fact you'd have let me go further, if I'd wanted.' He said the last words coldly.

'But you didn't want me, did you?' she asked and it was a statement rather than a question. 'You've never wanted me, Tony. I made a fool of myself three years ago. I'm older and wiser now. I haven't been chasing you at all—whether subtly or otherwise. I've hoped we could be friends but it seems to be impossible. I'm sorry, because I'm a friendly type of person and one can't have bad feeling in a camp like Blair—it affects the general atmosphere so quickly. It's merely your superlative conceit which makes you think I've been interested in you for any other reason.' She rose to her feet. 'I meant to apologize for slapping your face—now I only wish I'd done it before and a great deal harder!'

He rose too and faced her. Their eyes met, both hostile and angry. Who knows what angry words might have been spoken at that moment, words that would always be unforgivable and unforgotten, but Johnny came running up the steps to the pool and hailed them both. He had not witnessed the scene in the ballroom and he had been looking for Tony for the last few minutes.

'I wondered where the devil you were,' he said lightly as he came up to them. 'Am I interrupting a heart-to-heart talk?' He grinned at Gail and slipped his arm about her waist. 'I thought you kept those for me, Gail.'

'What's up?' Tony asked curtly.

'Nothing—except that the band are playing the last waltz and it's time for Goodnight Campers,' Johnny told him. 'The old man is wandering about the ballroom and he's sure to miss you if you aren't there for the last few minutes.'

Tony hurried away and ran down the steps. Gail and Johnny followed more slowly. He looked down at her, his arm still round her. 'Anything wrong?' he asked, puzzled by her silence and pallor. Quickly he said, 'Don't tell me you've been rowing with Tony again!'

She forced a smile. 'Of course—we've both come to the conclusion that we are natural enemies. In future, we shall studiously avoid each other.'

Johnny shook his head. 'I shall never

understand you two,' he said ruefully. 'I can't make you appreciate what a splendid fellow Tony is beneath the superficial façade that everyone else sees. I think I know him better than anyone—I only wish you could know him as well.'

Gail laughed briefly. 'Oh, I know him very well,' she said curtly. 'The more I know about him, the less I like him—but perhaps that's because I'm a woman and don't appreciate the qualities which appeal to men.'

As soon as they entered the ballroom, she saw Howard. He saw her at the same moment and came across to her. She felt a slight sinking of the heart, for his eyes were troubled and his step purposeful.

CHAPTER FOURTEEN

Gail hated the humiliation of making her apology to Tony. If those bitter words had not been spoken between them beside the swimming-pool, it would have been easy to apologize of her own volition as regret overcame pride. No doubt Tony would have accepted the apology in the spirit with which it was given. But when both knew that Howard was behind the apology, it was obviously insincere and therefore of little use to heal the breach between them.

Howard had heard the story as soon as he entered the ballroom that night. It was the subject of lively discussion and, catching a word or two here and there, he demanded the full story. He was disturbed and annoyed. Gail could do no wrong in his eyes—nor could Tony who was just as favoured—but he was equally annoyed with both of them for the scene in front of the campers. Anything that disturbed the happy equilibrium of the camp was a disaster in his eyes. It was their business if Gail and Tony wished to quarrel, but he preferred them to do so out of sight and hearing of the campers.

He was kind and firm with Gail when he approached her that evening. Whilst allowing that she probably had justification for her action, he pointed out the folly of putting the whole camp in a furore. If she apologized to Tony and let it be generally known that she had done so, then be seen with him on the best of friendly terms, the whole thing would blow over as a mild tiff and be forgotten within hours.

He spoke to Tony on similar lines and with a tightening of his lips Tony agreed to the suggestion.

Howard looked on with a satisfied expression as Gail went up to Tony, in full view of everyone in the ballroom, at the close of the dance. Goodnight Campers had just finished and the dancers were swarming on the ballroom floor. They watched eagerly as Gail spoke to Tony. Her words were too low to be heard by anyone but him, but the handshake which passed between them was obvious enough. Their smiles seemed natural enough and when Tony bent down to kiss her cheek murmurs of approval broke out through the ballroom. Several people chorused good-night to them both as they stood together, Tony's arm casually about her shoulders, talking lightly to a crowd of campers who had surged forward to find out what it was all about in the first place. They passed it off as a mere bagatelle and everyone seemed satisfied. At the first opportunity, Tony dropped his arm and turned away to talk to Paul and the other band-boys. Gail walked across to Howard and he greeted her with a warm smile as if to emphasize that all was forgiven and now would speedily be forgotten. As it was, the campers' brief week at the camp was all too short and packed with other things to occupy their minds and energies. They accepted the public apology at its face value and thought no more about the scene.

In the days that followed it was not so difficult for Gail to avoid Tony. It never is when the person you seek to avoid is just as concerned with avoiding you too.

The weather was dull and wet and Gail concentrated on her work in the office. As though sensing that Gail was not very happy, Johnny tried to spend more time with her, and she appreciated the generosity of his nature even more.

It rained heavily during the week and this meant providing the campers with indoor entertainment. Both Tony and Johnny were kept very busy. Tony welcomed the extra work, throwing himself into his duties with keen vigour and enthusiasm. Perhaps it needed more effort than formerly, but such was his personality and easy charm that this was not obvious to those who did not know him very well. He could not understand why he felt so despondent when he was alone or off duty and could relax his constant guard. His was a buoyant personality, but he was sometimes prey to moods of depression and irritation.

Never so much as now, and it was natural to connect it with his disagreement with Gail. He forced himself not to think about her or the angry words that had split asunder their precarious relationship. But it puzzled him that it should be an effort and not something which he could shrug aside with ease. He saw her about the camp, of course, but he did not seek her out and if they were in the same place he made no attempt to speak or smile. Their paths seldom crossed during the day. If he wished to check anything, he invariably sent Johnny to the office for the information. In the evenings he was busy and he tried to concentrate on the work in hand, but he all too frequently saw Gail dancing or standing at the bar with various people or crossing the ballroom to speak to different campers. That she was popular was very evident. It was not only her piquant beauty or the slender grace of her figure. She possessed an impulsive and friendly charm which quickly won her liking from everybody. Tony watched her and noticed these things and dwelt on them as he lay in the cool darkness of his chalet at night before sleep claimed him. Would it have been easier in the first place to acknowledge their former association and to renew the friendship? He had been afraid of the intensity of her youthful emotions and was sure at the time that he had done the right thing to show a cool hand. Now he admitted that he would value her friendship and her affection—purely on a friendly basis, of course—but it was too late. Too much water had passed beneath the bridge and they could never salvage anything from the ruins of their relationship. Better to let it go at that and not make a fool of himself . . .

Gail neatly rebuffed the young Ted at her first opportunity and he sought consolation from another girl who was a camper. At the end of the week, he went and other campers arrived. The days passed swiftly, despite her deep unhappiness. It hurt her anew every time she saw Tony and noticed his complete disinterest in her. She did not blame him for that. She had wanted to hurt him as he had hurt her—whether she had succeeded or not, at least he left her severely alone and there was no likelihood of any more hurtful words being spoken. She did not seek Tony out at all. Instead she turned more and more to Johnny and never found him wanting.

Johnny was kind and generous and affectionate. He was in love with Gail—deeply in love for the first time and, possibly, the last time in his life. But he had realized long ago where her heart lay and he was quite resigned to the hopelessness of his love. It was just as well that he was not cut out for marriage: he was too restless, too volatile, too fond of the opposite sex in a perfectly harmless way. He had no intention of committing himself where

Gail was concerned; for he was no fool, but a very shrewd young man. Impetuousness had never been one of his faults, although he thoroughly enjoyed mild flirtation and the company of women. At a very early age he had been engaged to a determined girl with her eye on the altar with whom he had originally been indulging in a hectic flirtation. Things had got beyond his control and developed by leaps and bounds. It had been a very narrow escape for him and as he had never loved her, even for the briefest fraction of time, he always considered himself fortunate to have escaped marriage. Ever after he checked his romantic and wayward tongue, managing to impart quite a lot with his expressive eyes and smile, but never committing himself.

Knowing that Gail loved Tony, he could not understand the enmity between them. At every opportunity he endeavoured to heal the breach but met with coolness on both sides. In vain, he talked of Gail to Tony with warmth and admiration, trying to impress on his friend what a sweet and generous person she was. Tony merely changed the subject. It was just as difficult to speak to Gail about Tony. It puzzled him that she spoke of him with dislike and anger when he knew so well how she really felt about Tony. Sometimes Johnny felt like telling her frankly that she was being foolish, that she should go to Tory of her own volition and tell him honestly that she loved him. No man could surely be immune to a woman like Gail under those circumstances. It might be the shake-up that Tony needed. Johnny had his own ideas about Tony's recent low spirits when off duty, but he had no intention of putting them into words for anyone's benefit. Realizing that it served no purpose to worry about the state of affairs between Gail and Tony, Johnny finally gave up trying to bring them together and merely concentrated on bringing back the sunny smile to Gail's lips and the happiness which she had once radiated all the time.

Suddenly, to his surprise, she took up with Graham, the young and attractive barman. It both surprised and pained him, for he had thought that she found a certain happiness and enjoyment in his company during her free time. What did Graham offer her?

Gail did not know herself why she had at last accepted an invitation to go into Midleigh with Graham. Since the season began, he had occasionally pressed her for a date and she had always refused in her charming way with the warm smile which made the refusal acceptable and gave Graham hope to try another time. He had been attracted to her on sight and it had piqued him that he wasn't having any success with her. He was personable enough for it to be unusual and it annoyed him that his friends knew of his failure and mocked him over it. Nevertheless, he remained attracted to

Gail—probably because of the lack of interest on her side. It was usually quite the opposite and Graham had developed a faint contempt for women because of their eagerness to befriend him. He was quite popular with the staff and Gail knew quite a lot about him which she had learned from Ann who had been out with him occasionally.

She was dispirited and a little bored with the camp and its occupants on the evening when Graham bought her a drink at the bar and then suggested that she go with him to Midleigh on the following afternoon. It was her free day and she knew that his afternoons were always free once the bar closed. She heard herself accepting and realized immediately that the words had slipped from her without any conscious effort on her part. But Graham looked so pleased that she didn't have the heart to tell him that she really didn't wish to go with him.

He had the reputation of being conceited and confident. He gave this impression with his manner and his extremely good looks. When Gail met him on the following afternoon outside the Reception Block, she was surprised to find him a little diffident.

'I'm afraid we'll have to take a bus,' he said. 'My old wreck has finally let me down. Do you mind?'

'No, of course not,' Gail returned. 'Why should I?'

Graham shrugged. 'I expect you're used to cars on your dates,' he said. 'Blair's, Tony's, Johnny's . . . I've seen you in them all.' He smiled. 'You're very popular Gail.'

'Johnny hasn't got a car,' she objected, a little taken aback by his apparent knowledge of her movements.

'Oh well—the camp car then. Everyone calls it Johnny's car,' he pointed out. The bus drew up before she could answer him. They sat on the top deck and he talked to her about the beauties of the countryside they passed through. She found him an interesting conversationalist. Not once did he mention the camp or the staff and this was a relief in itself. Gail sometimes tired of the fact that most of the staff could talk of nothing else.

When they reached Midleigh they went directly to the promenade and set out on the walk to the top of the cliff. Sitting on the grass with Graham, Gail was reminded of the many times she and Johnny had climbed the cliff walk and enjoyed the quiet peace at the top, facing towards the camp. But Graham turned his back on the camp and did not mention it at all. Instead he talked to her about his family and his home, his education, his ambitions to be an artist and travel abroad, his impatience with people who were always in a hurry and never took the time to appreciate the beauty in those things around them.

Gail said at last: 'I never thought you were

this type of person, Graham.'

He smiled. He had a particularly sweet smile and it gave his features an air of vulnerability. Gail felt the familiar impulse of affection sweep over her and she was glad. 'Because I serve behind the bar?' he asked. 'It's a job,' he went on. 'My family don't have much money. I'm studying at the London School of Art and I took this job during the summer to pay my fees. Lots of us are students. Didn't you know?'

'Oh yes, I knew that,' she returned quickly. It was true. 'But I didn't associate you with an appreciation of beauty or an inclination for art. You're a much different person away from the camp,' she added.

He shrugged. 'Aren't we all?' he asked obliquely. 'Holiday-camp life demands a façade—you've only to watch the campers and you can see that they too wear a façade for the short time they're here. Hail fellow well met— then back to their ordinary lives and they won't even condescend to speak to the neighbours.' He laughed shortly. 'People are really very odd.' He glanced at her and again that sweet smile. 'I didn't expect to be able to talk to you about myself so easily, Gail. I'm usually very close where my personal life is concerned. You're a sympathetic listener—I suppose that's the explanation.'

Gail brushed back a strand of dark hair which the breeze was toying with. It was a natural, beautiful gesture and the artist in Graham regretted that he did not have the materials to capture the scene. 'I think that's likely to be my epitaph,' she said lightly. 'I've been told so many times that I'm a good listener.'

'I've been told a great many things about you,' he said slowly. Gail stiffened. His eyes were candidly reassuring as he took her hand and turned it over between his slender fingers. He was fully aware of the tension in her. She had never noticed before how sensitive his hands were and it seemed incongruous to think of him pulling beer levers and handling beer and wine glasses. As he held her hand gently, she felt tension leaving her and relaxation seeping in. It was odd that a man she hardly knew could bring such peace to her troubled mind and spirit. But she felt as though she knew Graham very well. 'I must be about the only person in the camp who has never believed any of them,' he added quietly and she was touched by the sincerity in his voice.

'Thank you for that,' she said warmly and her hand tightened about his fingers.

He was diffident again. She realized that a shy streak ran through his nature and she thought of him with tenderness. 'Will you go out with me occasionally, Gail—could we be friends?' he asked. He added quickly: 'Of course you're always friendly enough, anyway—but I mean more than just casual acquaintances who happen to work in the same place. So few people are sensitive enough to make good companions for a man like me.' There was no conceit behind the words. 'I think you understand that I need to talk to someone about things that matter sometimes.' He smiled at her, searching her eyes. 'No strings attached,' he assured her quietly.

For answer she leaned forward impulsively and kissed him lightly. 'Of course, Graham. I know exactly what you mean.' A tiny sigh escaped her. 'I often feel the need of someone who won't make demands on me, too.'

His fingers tightened over hers but no more. He understood fully why she had kissed him and he did not attach anything to it which she did not intend.

When they returned to the camp she found him to be the same confident Graham behind the bar, his eyes quick to admire any pretty girl, his conversation light and shallow. But she understood now that with him it was all a convincing façade. She was glad that she had been given the chance to know the man underneath.

CHAPTER FIFTEEN

Graham was not in the least demanding. Whereas, when she was with Johnny, she was always conscious that he was fonder of her than was really wise, and whenever she was with Tony, she knew that active dislike was once more kindled into flame, Graham was a relaxing influence upon her. They found so much in common and, despite his reputation in the camp, she trusted him implicitly. He never attempted to kiss her with passion. Occasionally he fleetingly brushed her lips or her cheek or pushed back a lock of her dark hair with a tender gesture, but Gail knew that he was not in love with her or she with him. They were friends—and their friendship was of that type that insensitive people cannot appreciate. She did not neglect Johnny, but he was always busy and the bar hours allowed Graham a good deal of free time. Whenever possible, Gail slipped away from the office for an hour in the afternoon and they would walk through the surrounding countryside or go down to the beach. They seldom stayed in the camp, for the staff were too ready to comment upon their friendship. Gail found that she could talk easily and at great length to Graham on subjects that had hitherto only been active in her mind.

More than a little hurt by Gail's continued association with the barman, Johnny at last spoke of it to Tony.

'I can't understand what she sees in the man,' he lamented over drinks in the bar that evening. He glanced with some venom in Graham's direction. Gail was by the bar, talking to Graham when he was not serving, and apparently oblivious to the presence of the two organizers only a few yards away.

Tony shrugged. 'It's not your affair,' he said coolly.

'I feel concerned about her,' Johnny said. 'She's so damn trusting, somehow. I've tried to warn her about Graham, but she merely says that he isn't at all the sort of person that everyone thinks he is.' He laughed shortly. 'Women can be so gullible.'

'She's certainly trusting,' Tony said grimly. He turned his head to look at Gail and he was startled by the violence of his feelings as she laughed up at Graham in reply to a remark the man made. 'Still, she's old enough to choose her own friends, Johnny, and it doesn't do any good to worry about her. Anyway, I doubt if she's worth worrying about.'

Johnny stubbed his cigarette with a vicious movement. 'Don't be so blind! I don't know of a more worthwhile person than Gail. Any fool can see that.'

'Any fool perhaps, but I'm a fairly intelligent male,' Tony retorted.

Johnny glanced at him and his eyes were strangely enigmatic. 'For a fairly intelligent man, you're the biggest fool of them all, Tony. Why don't you bring your head out of the sand and come to your senses?'

'I don't know what you're talking about.' But Tony flushed slightly.

'That's exactly the trouble,' Johnny replied cryptically. His spirits rose. Now that he had confided his fears for Gail in somebody else, he began to wonder if most of them weren't merely imagined. Anyway, he trusted Tony not to repeat anything he had said and certainly he wasn't likely to do anything about it. He drained his beer and rose. 'Duty calls, old man. See you around.' The catchphrase came automatically.

Tony grinned. 'Shut up for the Lord's sake. I'm not one of your beloved campers.' He watched Johnny walk away and there was a spring to his step as though he was the lighter for having passed on his burden of anxiety. Tony toyed idly with his beer glass. Johnny was worrying himself unnecessarily over Gail's welfare. She was quite capable of taking care of himself—but the little thought nagged at him that she was indeed too trusting. One day she'd find herself in trouble through that inborn innocence which shone from her eyes— the one thing, the one facet of her personality, which always tormented him with doubts of the fairness of the gossip about her. Graham

183

had a reputation and Tony believed it to be justified. He wondered how involved she was with him, remembering her impulsive ways and that foolish innocence.

All evening he could not brush away the thought of her and Graham together. Johnny's words came back to bother him and eventually he knew that he must ease his own mind if no one else's. He went across to the bar and waited until Graham came up to him.

'Can I have a few words with you privately?' he asked, trying to keep the curtness from his voice.

'Sure!' Graham told him. 'Not much privacy here, but people are too interested in their own conversations to listen to ours.' He grinned and Tony felt a mild distaste for the man's confident air. He did not wish to discuss Gail in these surroundings, but also he did not wish to excite too much comment by taking Graham outside the ballroom.

'You're paying Gail Anson a great deal of attention these days,' he began.

'So?'

Tony knew it would be difficult to keep his temper but it was essential, so he kept his voice low as he replied: 'So I envy you. She's a sweet girl.' It was important not to antagonize Graham or he would never know anything.

'I didn't think you realized it,' Graham said slowly. 'From what she tells me, you two aren't exactly on friendly terms.'

'I imagine that you two are on terms far removed from friendly, knowing you.' Tony spoke lightly and flashed a man-to-man glance at Graham.

Graham flushed. 'Then you're quite wrong,' he said quietly. 'She doesn't come to any harm with me—if that's your worry.'

Tony looked his surprise. 'I wasn't talking about harm,' he said. 'But I've heard she's quite a girl when you get her on your own.'

Graham leaned on the bar and spoke softly. 'I believe you know quite a lot about Gail without pumping me. She's told me that you two used to know each other some time ago— surely you know how much importance to attach to the gossip that goes around the camp about her?' He looked about him and then spoke quieter still. 'Gail is a very sweet person and a very trusting one. Any man who would betray that trust must be pretty low. There's nothing between Gail and me but friendship— I hope that relieves your mind, Tony. If you wanted to know the truth about our association, why the devil didn't you ask me openly. It wasn't necessary to leer at me over the bar and insinuate that Gail's morals aren't all they should be.' He turned away and went to the farther end of the bar to serve a camper.

Thoughtfully, Tony stood with his back to the bar and surveyed the ballroom, but he scarcely saw the scene. He certainly did not hear the greeting of a camper who stood beside him. The camper was surprised, but he shrugged and gave his order to the barman, assuming the organizer to be concentrating on some entertainment problem. Tony did not like the feeling of foolishness as he recalled his hints to Graham about his association with Gail. Graham had known immediately what he wanted to know and had told him without demur or embarrassment. Now, of course, he would pass on the gist of the conversation to Gail, who would be furious that Tony should question their association. He shrugged philosophically. The breach between them could scarcely be wider, anyway.

Where had he gone wrong, he wondered, that he seemed to know less about the real Gail than anyone else who bothered to form a friendship with her? Was it merely that the angry quarrel had blinded him to her real qualities, for he had always defended her against malicious talk and insinuations before then? How would they end up—still enemies with that sea of dislike between them or simply indifferent to each other? Ruefully, he told himself that dislike was preferable to indifference. Gathering his wandering thoughts, he turned to the camper by his side and spoke easily to him, pushing Gail from his mind for the time being.

Howard Blair was well aware that the public apology which Gail had made to Tony had made little or no difference to the antagonism between them. Why they had quarrelled was none of his business and he did not seek to know. That they had quarrelled was the factor which disturbed him. He was sure in his own mind that Gail liked Tony and he could see no reason why the young organizer should not return that liking. He noticed that they very rarely spoke to each other these days and his great affection for Gail gave him an insight into her unhappiness. He longed to ease the situation, but saw no way of doing so. As always, he took the problem to Clare who was his adviser on many things. They worked together well and he knew that he owed much to her flair for organization and her keen efficiency. He was a little doubtful if either of these virtues could help him with the problem of Gail and Tony, but at least it eased his mind to discuss it with Clare.

They dined together. The meal was enjoyable and Howard kept the conversation on general topics throughout the time they sat at table. They took their coffee on the terrace and it was then, sitting close together, content in each other's company, that they saw Gail returning from an expedition with Johnny. It was Thursday evening. Howard frowned a little and glanced at his watch. Although it was Johnny's free day, he was usually back at the camp by six and he wondered idly where they had been that they returned so late. Gail looked towards the bungalow and she waved as she caught sight of her uncle and Clare on the terrace. It was a light-hearted wave and Howard felt a glow of relief that she seemed happy. Johnny parked the camp car while Gail waited for him outside the Reception Block which was in full view from the terrace. Then they walked together, hands linked, and Gail looked back once more towards the bungalow as if aware that they were being watched.

Taking his opportunity, Howard said softly. 'You know, Clare, I'm rather worried about Gail.'

Clare smiled reassuringly. 'Unnecessarily so, I feel sure. Gail can take care of herself.'

'Oh, of course. I'm not worried in that sense,' he hastened to explain. 'I suppose you know—most people do—that she and Tony had one hell of a row recently?'

Clare nodded. 'And you suggested that Gail should apologize to Tony in full view of the campers—yes, I do know, Howard.'

Ht looked at her quickly. 'That rather sounds as if you disapproved.'

Clare was silent for a moment. Then she nodded. 'I don't usually interfere with your judgment, Howard,' she said quietly, 'but I do think you were wrong for once. I'm quite sure that Gail would have apologized to Tony in her own good time—and much more sincerely. I couldn't see at the time what good a public apology did.'

Howard frowned, stubbing his cigarette in

the ashtray which stood on the small table at his side. 'I couldn't let the campers think that there was any disharmony among the staff. You know as well as I do that the slightest thing can strain the atmosphere in a place like a holiday camp—and everyone senses it.'

'Well, I think that you drew more attention to the incident by insisting on the public apology. It would have blown over very quickly of its own accord—and Tony and Gail would possibly have remained good friends.'

'One could scarcely give that name to their relationship in the first place,' Howard demurred. 'After all, there's been a certain amount of antagonism between them since Gail first came here.'

'Yes—and they've not had a chance to find out the good in each other,' Clare told him sharply.

Howard went on to what was really troubling him. 'I wish there were something I could do,' he said slowly. 'Some way to bring them together—if only for Gail's sake.' He said abruptly, 'It's my guess she cares more for Tony than she'll ever admit, Clare.'

'There's nothing you can do—and I think they'd both resent any interference. Johnny, for instance, is always trying to get Tony to accept Gail and I expect he talks to Gail like a Dutch uncle.' She smiled briefly. 'Now he's a fine young man. I like Johnny very much. He's the type who would push aside his own

189

happiness if he could do something for his friends. I think we must let Gail sort out her own life, Howard. She's not a child. If she does care for Tony, then she'll find her own way of making things up with him. As for Tony,' she sighed a little, 'much as I like him, I still think he's a very difficult character. Proud as Lucifer, as stubborn as a mule when he chooses, and sometimes as blind as a bat when he's afraid of what he'll see.'

Howard smiled at her and there was more than just admiration in his eyes for the shrewd woman who saw so much more than she ever mentioned. 'Clever Clare,' he said quietly. 'I've been turning over ideas of having a quiet word with the pair of them and trying to help them to sort out their differences. You make me realize that I'd be like a bull in a china shop. I'm not always very good at handling other people's affairs, but unfortunately I don't always realize it until I've made matters worse.' He laid his hand over hers.

Clare left her hand in his clasp but she did not meet his eyes. Instead she looked towards the camp and he could not read her expression as she said quietly, 'You're not very good at handling your own affairs sometimes, are you, my dear?' She felt the instinctive surprise reflect in the pressure of his fingers.

'My own affairs?' he questioned and his voice was very low.

Clare knew that he was aware of what was

190

in her mind. A smile flickered at her lips. 'Well, you've been wanting to ask me to marry you for weeks—and still you can't speak the actual words.' She turned her head now and smiled at him. Their eyes met and he read the encouragement and affection which she offered in her expression. The hot colour surged into his face and he felt like a young lad caught in the heady throes of first love and choked with shyness. Taking pity on his embarrassment, Clare went on easily, 'I've known for ages. I think I knew before you did what was in your mind. I'm not a fool, Howard, and I soon noticed the subtle difference in your feelings for me.'

'You must think I'm a fool,' he managed to say.

Clare laughed gently. 'Why—because you want to make me an honourable proposal? My dear Howard, I'm very touched—and complimented.'

He caressed her fingers absently. 'Of course I realize it's out of the question, Clare—but one always hopes . . .'

'It isn't out of the question. I'm only waiting for you to ask me and then I shall gladly accept. But I certainly don't intend to put any more words into your mouth,' she teased him affectionately. She watched his expression change from diffidence to astonishment.

'Then you do care for me?'

She admonished him with a shake of her

head. 'I don't mean to give anything away at this stage of the game.'

'You sweet devil!' he chided her. 'Clare, I'm madly in love with you—it sounds so damn silly at my age but it's true enough. Will you marry me, Clare?'

'Gladly,' she told him. Leaning forward, she kissed him softly on the mouth. He raised a hand to stroke her hair.

'Dare I hope that you're a little fond of me?' he asked.

'More than a little,' she replied warmly. 'I love you very much, Howard—and I thought you'd never do anything about it unless I pushed you into it.'

He rose and drew her into his arms where she rested at peace, her head on his shoulder. 'You didn't have to push me, darling,' he said gently. 'But I've been afraid—I mean, you told me about Bob and how happy you were with him. You loved him so much. Naturally, I never thought I had a chance. I'm a deal older than you and not very exciting.'

She raised her head to smile up at him. 'I don't want excitement, Howard—just contentment and happiness. You can offer so much more than that, anyway. Yes, I loved Bob dearly and almost broke my heart when he died. But I've never regretted those few months of exciting bliss. Now I'm old enough to appreciate other things—companionship, sincere friendship, kindness and courtesy, staunch affection. You've always given me those things.'

'I wish I could give you the world,' he declared in the age-old impetuosity of lovers.

Clare shook her head and laughed gently. 'I don't want the world—only the small part of it which we can share, my dearest.'

Then he kissed her and thought that it was the first time he had ever held her close and pressed his lips to hers although they had been close friends for so many years. When their lips parted, he said quietly, 'I've wasted so much time. I wonder why it took me so long to realize that I wanted you, Clare.'

'Possibly because I only realized a few months ago that I wanted you,' she told him quietly. Then she raised herself up to kiss him.

Later they talked of their future life together and Clare was amused to find how impatient he was for their marriage to begin. She was amused, because although he was a keen and shrewd business man and never hesitated to plunge into something which would bring him new success, in his private life he was both cautious and uncertain of success. Now, sure of their future happiness, he was impatient and fired Clare with some of his own eagerness.

CHAPTER SIXTEEN

To celebrate his engagement to Clare Marshall, which was announced the following day, Howard ordered that every drink bought that day was on the camp. He was inundated with congratulations from staff and campers alike.

Gail was particularly delighted. She had often wondered why her charming and kindly uncle had never married, for he was so obviously cut out to be a family man. She liked Clare and admired her qualities and it was not difficult to realize why Howard wanted her for his wife. Clare was generally popular and during the next few days it seemed very true that all the world loves a lover, for the whole camp was talking about the engagement and wishing the couple well.

Ann claimed that she had prophesied the event long ago and was frankly pleased with her own perspicacity. 'They've always been such friends,' she said to Gail in the privacy of their chalet. 'I expected them to make a match of it ages ago.' She laughed. 'I suppose Howard didn't really like the idea of a change in his domestic affairs—men of his age are so staid.'

'There's nothing staid about Howard,' defended Gail stoutly. 'I expect he thought

Clare was faithful to the memory of her dead husband.'

Ann raised an eyebrow. 'Life's too short for that kind of thing. If ever I'm widowed, I shall look around immediately for another meal ticket!'

'You've got to find the first husband yet,' Gail reminded her lightly, ignoring Ann's vulgarity. She often came out with such philosophies, but Gail knew that it was mere idle chatter rather than her ideas on life. 'I shall be surprised if any man ever wants to take you on.'

Ann looked vaguely mysterious. 'Oh, I won't make such a bad wife for the right man, Gail.'

'You sound as though you've someone in mind.'

'Perhaps I have.' Gail looked up sharply at these words. 'Perhaps I have,' Ann repeated slowly.

'Anyone I know?' Gail asked, trying to keep the swift fear from her voice. 'Not Tony, by any chance?'

Ann smiled. 'Why should it be Tony? Don't sound so scared, my sweet—I've no intentions of stealing him from you.

'Don't be absurd,' Gail retorted swiftly. 'Tony doesn't belong to me.'

'Do I detect a trace of regret?' Ann noticed the faint shadow in her friend's eyes and she added hastily, 'Oh, don't take any notice of me, Gail. You know how I run on. It isn't Tony, anyway. I'm not saying any more. My lips are sealed!' she declared dramatically.

Gail said lightly, 'Well, if you're going to announce an engagement in the near future, I hope you'll keep up the tradition and buy free drinks for all! Howard's created a precedent now!' Absently she added: 'I hope Clare won't expect me to call her "aunt" when they're married.' She forgot momentarily that Ann did not know of her relationship to Howard Blair.

Ann looked startled. It did not take much intelligence to arrive at the right conclusion. 'Do you mean that Howard's your uncle?' she asked in astonishment.

Gail bit her lip. 'That slipped out,' she said slowly. 'I forgot you didn't know—don't spread it around, Ann, please. I don't want the fact generally known here.'

Ann was delighted with the news. 'All right,' she promised lightly. 'But you are a dark horse, Gail. And I thought Howard was sweet on you when all the time he was just being the benevolent uncle.' She laughed. 'No wonder you get away with murder!'

'That isn't true!' objected Gail. 'I don't have preferential treatment. I wouldn't want it either.' She sounded quite distressed and Ann regretted her remark. She rumpled Gail's hair in a casual caress.

'Don't get heated. I didn't mean anything. But you must be really thrilled, Gail—I wonder if Clare will ask you to be a bridesmaid.'

Gail shook her head. 'I doubt it. I expect they'll have a very quiet wedding. Clare's a widow, for one thing, and Howard doesn't like undue ceremony.'

She went over to the bungalow that evening to see Howard. He had not been in the office all day and he had left a message for Gail that he was taking Clare to London. It did not take much stretch of the imagination to assume that they went in search of an engagement ring. Howard was in the lounge when Gail arrived and he moved forward to greet her. He looked ten years younger, Gail thought, and she wondered on the rejuvenating effect that love can have on people. Some people, she amended. Her love for Tony had only brought unhappiness and these days she felt much older than her actual years. Perhaps the secret lay in having one's love returned.

'There you are, Gail. I thought you'd be over. Well, what do you think of the news?' he asked eagerly, boyishly.

'I'm so pleased, Howard,' she said warmly. She threw her arms about him and hugged him with affectionate strength. 'I think Clare is a wonderful person—and you're both very lucky!'

He smiled. 'I think she's wonderful too. Come on to the terrace. Clare is showing off her ring to Tony.' He put his arm about Gail's shoulders. 'I expect you guessed why we went to London?'

Gail barely heard him. Her eyes were on Tony who stood on the terrace, lounging against the verandah post, smoking and talking to Clare. He turned as Howard came out with Gail. Their eyes met and his were cool, indifferent. Angry, she stiffened and her glance was sweeping and contemptuous. Then she hurried to Clare and smiled warmly. 'Let me see your ring! Congratulations, Clare—I think it's wonderful news. The whole camp is delighted . . .'

'The free drinks did the trick,' Howard put in, laughing.

Clare obediently proffered her left hand so that Gail could admire the large diamond solitaire which flashed and sparkled bravely. 'You don't mind having me in the family?' she asked lightly.

Gail threw her a reproachful glance. 'I should say not. It's high time Howard was married anyway.'

'That's what I keep telling Clare,' her uncle told her. 'Anyway, a drink! What will you have, Gail? Tony?' A little later, he said: 'Clare and I thought a small dinner party would be rather pleasant as a private celebration. Not many of us, of course. You, Gail, and Tony—Johnny, and I thought perhaps your chalet mate would care to join us to make the numbers even. Ann, isn't it?' He addressed Gail and she

198

nodded. 'There isn't anyone you'd like to invite, Gail? A particular friend, for instance?' He turned to Tony. 'How about you?'

Tony had been very quiet but it had not been noticeable for Gail and Clare had kept up the conversation and Howard was scarcely in a mood to notice anyone else's low spirits. Now Tony replied: 'I doubt if I can make the party, anyway, Blair. It's rather difficult in the middle of the season. If you want Johnny, then count me out.'

'As you wish.' Howard shrugged. He wondered briefly if Tony preferred to keep out of Gail's way. It was true that both organizers couldn't desert their work for one evening: he had forgotten for the moment. He would rather have Tony than Johnny, but he was willing to acquiesce to Tony's wishes.

Gail said suddenly: 'It would be nice if you'd invite Graham—he's a good friend of mine. I'm sure he could be spared from the bar for one evening.' She tilted her chin, aware that Tony's eyes were on her as she spoke.

'Graham? Isn't he the fair young man?' Howard asked. 'I think I know who you mean. Yes, all right, Gail my dear. That will be six of us then—three of each sex. Very nicely arranged. Shall we say tomorrow evening?' It was agreed and then Tony placed his empty glass on the table and said that he must be getting back to the ballroom. 'Already?' Howard asked regretfully. He sensed the strain between Gail and Tony and he was very disappointed. He had hoped that the brief half-hour over drinks and the convivial atmosphere would have helped to melt the frigidity of their relationship. But Tony had been aloof and Gail had not once spoken directly to him. Howard sighed a little. These young people did not seem to realize that life was too short for animosity to be upheld indefinitely. It was a pity that they could not tolerate each other even for a short while.

'So must I,' Gail said abruptly and impulsively. 'I'll pass on the invitation to Graham, shall I? I know he'll be pleased.' She knew that unless he meant to be deliberately rude, Tony could not avoid walking back to the ballroom with her if she left now. Possibly he would snub any approach she made, but she was prepared to take the risk. How long was it since they had spoken on friendly terms? She did not like to remember. She wished that he had shown even the slightest unbending during the last half-hour. Did he hate her so much that he had to make it obvious to everyone or was he merely completely indifferent to her presence. She had been tempted to speak to him naturally as though nothing had ever happened to cause a rift in their association but, afraid that he might snub her openly, she had checked her tongue.

Howard made no attempt to detain Gail for he, too, realized that the couple would walk back together and he was glad that Gail at least had the sense to attempt a reconciliation. For surely that was her motive, or she would have stayed on at the bungalow for a little longer and then left alone.

They crossed the lawns which surrounded the bungalow and stepped on to the roadway which led into the camp grounds. Then it was that Tony said coldly, 'Not very subtle—I thought you could do better than that!'

Colour stained her cheeks swiftly. 'I decided long ago that the subtle approach is useless with you, Tony. It's much better to be direct.'

'Why bother?' he sneered. 'You and I are poles apart—I'm happy to keep it that way.'

'Why are you always so unpleasant?' Her quick temper was roused instantly. 'You're charming enough to everyone else.'

'I keep it for my friends,' he said coldly.

'It sometimes pays to be nice to one's enemies, too,' she reminded him and her voice was just as icy. He made no reply and they walked along in hostile silence. Gail's heart sank. She regretted the impulse to accompany him and the hope that had gone with it. He was impossible! It seemed that he was determined not to lower his pride in any way. Agreed that she had wounded his pride badly, the least he could do was to accept the situation with a good grace and try to forget it. She reminded herself that he could not know how deeply involved her feelings were, but

201

even that was no excuse for his continual wish to hurt her. She wondered whether she should succumb to tears and perhaps win his sympathy—but she cast aside the thought almost before it was born. Tony was so unpredictable and he was likely to be even more contemptuous of her. She said bitterly, following up her thoughts: 'You won't even call a truce, will you?'

'What's the point?' he demanded. 'Every time we speak to each other we quarrel.' There was the faintest regret in his voice and she looked at him quickly, fresh hope springing to life. Perhaps after all he would really welcome something akin to friendship between them, she thought swiftly.

A rueful smile touched her lips. 'It's strange because I'm not really an argumentative type of person, Tony. I'd much rather be on friendly terms with everyone.'

'You're too friendly,' he accused. 'And you choose your friends unwisely.'

Gail stiffened, the smile fading. 'You can't mean Johnny or Ann,' she said slowly. 'I presume you mean Graham.'

'That's right,' he said stiffly.

'It's my business—and besides, you just don't know Graham. He's a wonderful friend—and a wonderful person. You're just deceived—as everyone is—by the façade.'

He shrugged. 'Trusting little fool!' It was not an endearment. 'Why do you always assume your judgment to be infallible?'

Gail bit her lip. 'I admit I was wrong about you,' she said hotly. 'You're conceited and stubborn and . . . and . . .'

'Not worth bothering about,' he finished for her, apparently unconcerned by her attack.

'And utterly lovable,' she finished silently and knew it was true despite the faults she threw at him. Aloud she said: 'I can't imagine why I ever liked you!'

He grinned mirthlessly. 'Because you endow people with all the virtues on first sight and then blame them if they don't live up to your ideal of them. Your standards are too high, Gail.'

'I aim high,' she said, tilting her chin proudly. 'I must have been fortunate for I've always found that people are as nice as I think—until you disillusioned me, anyway.'

He thrust his hands into his pockets. 'Three years ago—or this year?'

'Why do you ask that?' She was surprised by his question.

He shrugged. 'I'm wondering if your dislike of me dates from my lack of interest in you three years ago or from our recent quarrel.'

She hesitated a moment. Then she said in a low voice: 'Why do you assume that I dislike you, Tony? It isn't true, you know.'

He stopped short and the abrupt movement pulled Gail up. He looked down at her. 'You're not very consistent,' he said slowly. 'A few seconds ago you couldn't think of enough unpleasant things to attribute to me. Now you want me to believe that you like me despite everything.'

She met his eyes squarely. 'You just don't know what to believe. I've told you that before. Have you ever tried thinking about me with an open mind, Tony? When I first came here, you decided that you didn't want to recognize our previous friendship. That was unkind in itself. Then you deliberately snubbed me at every opportunity—and made a fool of me that day we went to the bay,' she added thoughtlessly.

'That wasn't my intention!' he exclaimed sharply.

She went on as though she hadn't heard him. 'Then that ridiculous quarrel—and you've made full use of the reason for avoiding me ever since. It seems that you've never wanted me here and resented my presence at the camp. Well, I'm sorry if you consider me a nuisance, but I happen to love my job and love the camp and I'm not leaving for you or anyone.' Her voice rose with the heat of her emotions. Suddenly inquiry came into her eyes. 'Did you ever try handing in your resignation? You said you intended to.'

He shook his head. 'My sentiments are the same as yours. I love this place and I'm not letting you drive me away. The camp can hold us both—as long as we keep away from each other.' He glared down at her. 'Don't create opportunities to be with me—you're wasting your time!'

The urge to slap his cheek again was upon her but Gail controlled it. Angry as she was, she strove to keep her temper. It cost her an effort but suddenly she held out her hand to him. 'Tony, won't you shake hands and be friends? Forget the past few weeks and let's try to get to know each other. A new start? Please.'

It was a generous gesture and he was startled. He looked at her small, outstretched hand and then he looked at the small face with the anxious eyes, the tremulous mouth and the determined chin. He did not know what to make of her. Again he was bewildered by the sudden turn of events, the unexpected facet of her character. No other woman had ever confused his impressions as Gail did. He did not like the feeling. But he knew that friendship with Gail was impossible. It was too mild a feeling—it must be either love or hate and he did not know which emotion flooded his entire being as he looked down at her. Suddenly he did not wish to know.

'Friends?' he queried with a world of bitterness behind the word. 'Not you and I, Gail—no!' He brushed her hand aside. 'What the devil do you hope to gain?' he demanded. 'Just what do you want from me, anyway?' It was a cry from the confused turmoil of his thoughts and emotions. Embarrassed and angry that she should have got beneath his control, he turned on his heel without waiting for her answer and walked away.

Gail watched his tall figure stride purposefully into the ballroom. Her heart felt as though it were being clutched by a cold and cruel hand. Tears would be a welcome release, but she had never felt less like crying. The pain went much deeper than that. Yet with the pain was a sense of triumph, the knowledge that she was forcing Tony to think of her with just more than superficial ease and casualness, the truth that far from being indifferent to her he was now unsure how he did feel about her. At least she was making some progress. She could forgive him for his ungraciousness and the cruel remarks, for she sensed that, like herself, he had been unhappy since their quarrel and certainly was in no contented frame of mind at this very moment. If he were indifferent to her, then he would not bother to quarrel with her every time they met and he would treat her lightly and casually—as he had done when she first came to the camp. Perhaps he hated her just now—but didn't someone once say that only a razor's edge divides hate from love? At times, Gail came near to hating Tony—but beneath the momentary anger always lived the deep and lasting emotion which was her love for him. She did not know why she loved him so much—but love was not easily explained. Certainly there was no doubt about the sincerity of her feelings: she was mature enough to be able to define affection as affection—and love as love. She had a great affection for Johnny and for Graham, but it was indeed love which dwelt in her being for Tony—obstinate, proud, handsome and charming Tony Sheppard.

CHAPTER SEVENTEEN

It was impossible to sleep. Tony turned restlessly, sat up and thumped his pillows, lay down again and tried to make his mind a blank. It was useless and he gave up the attempt to slip into blessed unconsciousness. He sat up, switched on the bedside lamp, and took a cigarette from the packet on the table by his bed. It was very quiet in the chalet lines. No doubt all the staff were in bed and sleeping peacefully, he thought bitterly. Damn all women! A thousand curses on their pretty, empty heads! Thank God he'd escaped the bonds and shackles of marriage! It was bad enough that a woman should torment him like this, by night as well as day—imagine being married to one and having to cope with their illogicality, the swift changes of mood, the demands. Why the devil couldn't Gail leave matters alone? Why did she keep trying to patch up a sinking ship? Did she think she could heal the breach with an outstretched hand and an offer of friendship after all that had gone before?

He was mixing his metaphors and the thought made him smile reluctantly. Poor Gail! He was surprised by the sudden surge of sympathy. He could have been gracious and accepted the peace offering. What on earth had made his control slip away from him like that? He was thankful that no one had witnessed the scene. All the campers had been in the ballroom and the staff were busy at that time.

He drew on his cigarette and then exhaled the smoke. He watched it wind and curl into nothingness and he thought suddenly that life was like that. Swift and pointless, swayed this way and that by the winds of chance and incidence, eventually ending in nothingness; he caught up his morbid thoughts. Perhaps not so pointless: he enjoyed life with all its problems and difficulties and rewards and he had chosen the one career which surely was worth while for a man like himself and truly satisfying; but it was certainly swift. He was almost thirty: young still and with much of his future still unplumbed. He moved restlessly. He wasn't very concerned with his future, as a rule. He was content to live in the present. But the future suddenly stretched before him and it seemed empty. He had many years at Blair Holiday Camp to anticipate, but that did not seem enough any longer. Gail! It was her fault that he knew this restlessness, this sense of emptiness in his life. She constantly invaded his thoughts. There were so many sides to her character—and many of them he had never seen. He thought again of her generous attempt to make peace with him. How many girls would do that? he wondered idly. Most would have accepted the situation and mentally dispatched him to Hell. She was an exasperating wretch with a core of sweetness and innocence and charm. His mind jerked backwards to the day when they had driven to the peaceful little bay and he had kissed her. The memory of her warm body beneath his hard chest, the eager ardency of her lips, his own strange half-shamed, half-triumphant emotions tormented him with vivid vitality. He felt again the same mixture of hate and love which had burned in his breast as he looked down at her only that afternoon. Hate and love—hate or love. What was it he felt for that trusting, generous and strangely appealing woman?

He stubbed his cigarette angrily and switched off the light. Refusing to think, he burrowed his dark head into the pillows—but the question came back a moment later. Hate or love? Did he hate her? No, of course not—she had too many good qualities. Who could possibly hate Gail with her piquant little face, the shining eyes, the kissable mouth, that chin with its determined tilt, the crop of dark curls which framed her face? She was suddenly so vivid before his closed eyes that he cursed again. If this violent, confusing and desperate emotion was love, then he wanted none of it. He rejected the idea scornfully. Love—he wasn't capable of it. If he were, he'd have loved many women in his time. God, he'd had the opportunities. But none had ever invaded his thoughts like this or made it impossible to control the forceful invasion. He groaned as his brain whirled again into a kaleidoscope of memories in which Gail figured prominently: a slender girl in a swimsuit diving from the edge of the pool; a furious whirlwind raising her hand to slap his face; an ardent yet innocent woman in his arms on the golden sands; a creation of piquant loveliness whirling on the dance floor in the arms of men she barely knew; a laughing imp hand in hand with Johnny as they raced over the green lawns; an aloof and vaguely sophisticated creature flirting with Graham as she stood at the bar in the ballroom, ignoring him and unconsciously paining him by that indifference.

So many different Gails. So many appealing sides to her character. Yet to him always the one side: angry, contemptuous, cold. Except for the rare moments when the real Gail shone through in moments of impulse, of warmth and friendliness, of humour.

Love tore and tortured him. Pain and anguish and longing beseiged him. He sought in his memory those few occasions when he had known the impulsive warmth and he clung to them like a drowning man to a raft. Perhaps she was not totally contemptuous of him. God knew he had never given her reason to think well of him! Regret and anger against himself swept through his entire being. One more chance! he thought desperately. Let Gail give him one more opportunity and he would make amends for his stupidity. Never again would he fan the cold ashes of their quarrel into fresh life with hard words and cold looks. If she would not give him a chance, then he would create his own. He thought of his own words to her that very day: *Don't create opportunities to be with me.* What a crass fool he had been and only now did he realize it. Now he would have to create opportunities to be with her and risk her scorn when he abased himself at her feet. Innocent, trusting Gail with all her loveliness and sweetness offered to him in friendship— more times than he cared to remember, for he had spurned her every time.

It was an ironic situation and he laughed, but there was no joy or humour in the sound. That this should happen to him when he thought himself immune from love and its effects. He had certainly never realized that love could be both a torment and an ecstasy, mingling pain and pleasure until it was impossible to know where one finished and the other began.

At last he slept, but his dreams were all of Gail and it was a restless night. With the fresh day came fresh determination to win Gail for his own, to erase the unpleasantness which had been between them for what now seemed an eternity, to make amends for his harshness and folly.

As Gail had anticipated, Graham accepted the invitation to join the dinner party at the bungalow. He was both pleased and touched, for he was aware that Gail's generosity was behind the invitation. She told him most things and he knew that she was Howard Blair's niece. He knew one other thing which she had never told him—that she loved Tony Sheppard, that her life revolved around the one man who seemed immune to her charms and loveliness, that he caused her much unhappiness. Graham felt a natural anger against Tony, but there had never been any love lost between them. He had not been surprised when Tony had asked him in a roundabout manner how far his association with Gail had gone. He was convinced that Tony's thoughts were more often with Gail than anyone realized, least of all Gail herself. It was a strange thing, this friendship that Graham had formed with Gail. It seemed to be a rare affinity, an appreciation of each other's company and conversation, an affection which owed nothing to love or passion which was probably the reason why the friendship remained on an even keel and was never misunderstood by either of them.

Gail went to the office the following morning and settled down to work, although she felt strangely restless. Her thoughts wandered to the dinner party that evening: from there they turned to Tony and his curt refusal to her offer of friendship. She sighed a little. She had tried so many times. She would not try again. The night before, trying to sleep, she had come to terms with her wilful heart which persisted in loving Tony. Her love would never alter, but at least she would prevent it from dominating her whole life. She would learn to live without basing a future on Tony: she would learn to accept their present animosity; she would learn to control her impulsive emotions and leave him severely alone. It was the only way to find peace of mind and perhaps one day she would be able to think of him, speak to him or walk with him, without her heart lurching uncontrollably and her tongue rushing her into hasty words that had no meaning behind them.

She bent her dark head over the typewriter and furiously rubbed away at a mistake. It was not the first mistake she had made that morning, for her mind was not on the list she copied. Every movement made her feel hot and uncomfortable, for it was a very warm day. The heat haze over the sea had been quite dense when she left her chalet for breakfast. It was clearing now and the sun was bright and strong. All the windows in the office were open but there was little breeze to stir the atmosphere. Gail could hear the music being broadcast over the Tannoy for the benefit of the campers and above it the gay shouts of people out in the sunshine and making the most of their brief holiday.

Tony paused by the open door and looked at her. His mouth was suddenly dry and his heart pounded furiously. Chiding himself for behaving like a callow youth, he stepped into the room and approached her desk, hoping he would appear casually at his ease, hoping she would not notice the tumult in his blood.

She looked up quickly. Tony was the last person she expected to see in her small office and she caught her breath.

He laid a sheaf of papers on her desk. 'Would you type two copies of this for me, Gail?' he asked. 'I'd like it today if it's possible.'

Gail picked up the papers and leafed through them. 'Can do,' she said lightly. Without looking at him, she reminded him: 'You usually send Johnny over with this kind of thing—running your own errands this morning?'

'Johnny was busy,' he said awkwardly. He perched on the edge of her desk and brought out his cigarettes.

'So am I,' she said. Picking up her eraser again, she rubbed furiously at the sheet of paper in the typewriter. Too furiously, for a hole appeared and angrily she wrenched the sheet from the machine.

Tony pushed the cigarette packet towards her. 'Have a breather for a few minutes,' he suggested. 'It doesn't look as though you're in

215

the mood for work today, anyway.'

Gail indicated the open windows and the blazing sunshine. 'Who would be on a day like this?' she demanded. She was surprised by the ease of his attitude, but she had no intention of allowing it to undermine the decisions she had made about him. She took a cigarette from the packet and bent her head over the match he struck into flame.

'Take the day off,' Tony suggested. 'Howard isn't a slave driver and he's so wrapped up in his romance at the moment he'd agree to anything.'

Gail tapped the sheaf of papers he had brought for typing. 'Then you wouldn't get this today, and I imagine it's urgent.'

Tony shrugged. 'Not that urgent.' He did not add that it had been merely an excuse to see her for a few minutes. He glanced obliquely at her face but it was composed and serene. She was not disturbed by his presence apparently. He wondered if she would be impetuous enough to mention their argument the day before.

There was silence between them. Gail searched her brain for some casual remark but found none. Neither could she find an explanation for his presence and his evident inclination to stay a while.

He asked inanely: 'Are you looking forward to the dinner party tonight?'

Grateful for some subject of conversation,

Gail said brightly: 'Very much. Howard knows how to throw a good party even if it will be a small one.' She added: 'A pity you can't make it, Tony.'

'Graham accepted, I suppose?'

'Of course. He was very pleased too. I think he'll be an excellent addition to the gathering. He can be very amusing, you know.'

'Anything serious between you two?' Tony heard himself ask abruptly. He toyed with his cigarette, turning it over and over in his fingers.

Gail played with various gadgets on her typewriter. 'You've already had your answer to that question from Graham, I believe.'

Tony felt a surge of annoyance. So Graham had passed on their conversation. He had expected him to do so, but it still annoyed him to find that he had mentioned it to Gail. 'I had his answer,' he returned. 'I'm asking you now?'

She gave him a mischievous glance. Her spirits rose that he should be so interested in her association with Graham. Was there a touch of jealousy behind his interest? 'We're just good friends,' she said lightly and her eyes were laughing.

Meeting those laughing eyes, his heart leaped. How variable she was! One moment solemn and serious, the next gay and vivacious. One would never know with Gail—she was unpredictable, that was the word—like the English weather, he thought, with grim humour.

'The time-honoured tag,' he mocked, answering lightness with lightness. 'I thought you'd be more original.'

'It just happens to be the truth.' Gail assured him. 'Is it so hard to believe that I could have a firm and innocent friendship with a man?'

'I've never believed much in platonic associations,' he said. 'But you've a very convincing manner. I'll take your word for it.'

She raised her eyebrows. 'I can't imagine you taking my word for anything, Tony.'

He glanced down again at his cigarette. 'I guess I've misjudged you quite a lot at times.'

'Is that the nearest thing to an apology I can expect from you?' she asked him coolly, but her heart leapt.

'It's an apology of sorts. Take it or leave it!' he said sharply. Then quickly the spurt of temper faded. He grinned at her disarmingly. 'You're an exasperating wretch, Gail— sometimes I could cheerfully throttle you.'

'It doesn't take much to rouse your fury where I'm concerned,' she reminded him.

'No,' he admitted. He added lightly, 'If ever you marry a man like me, Gail, you'd lead one hell of an existence—fighting one minute, kissing the next!'

She glanced at him from beneath long lashes and her eyes were provocative. Her heart was beating unsteadily and sweet fire ran

218

through her veins. Throwing caution to the winds, she said slowly: 'I've fought often enough with you, Tony, but I've not had much evidence of the kissing.'

He dropped his cigarette to the floor and stepped on it. He met Gail's eyes and his own were dark and full of promise. 'That could be remedied, you know.'

Gail made no reply, her eyes still holding his. She caught her breath as he moved slightly towards her. In a moment she would have been crushed in his arms, but a warning voice in his brain told him that this was not the way. If he kissed her now because of her provocative invitation, she would only link his motives with those that had led him to kiss her on the golden sands of the bay. She would not understand that there was a world of difference between his feelings then and now. With an effort he controlled the wild tumult of desire and longing. Damn those provocative eyes and the sweet lips which had been etched for kissing! Holding on to his control, he walked over to the window. Gail studied the taut back, the dark head and broad shoulders. Why had he not kissed her then? She knew with all the instincts of a woman that the intention had been in his eyes and his blood and his movement towards her. What had prevented him? The old fear that she would misinterpret his kisses and imagine him in love with her? Or a reluctance to kiss her casually merely because she had offered a blatant invitation? Or was it possible—and the thought stilled her heartbeat for a fraction of time—that he was afraid of giving his emotions away if he kissed her? A kiss could tell so much and perhaps Tony wanted to keep his secrets to himself. Gail longed to know the truth, but she did not dare to ask.

Casually, he said, forcing his voice to remain light and steady: 'It really is a lovely day, Gail—you'll surely take a couple of hours this afternoon and get out into the sun?'

Gail inserted a sheet of paper into her typewriter. 'I think so—Howard usually insists on it when the weather is good.'

He moved towards the door. 'I'll see you later. Perhaps you'd bring those papers to my office when you take your free time?'

When he had gone, Gail stared unseeingly out of the window, her work forgotten . . .

CHAPTER EIGHTEEN

Tony waited impatiently. There was work that needed attention on his desk: within a very short time he would have to leave his office and concentrate on the campers. He glanced at his watch. Surely Gail would arrive soon with those damn papers! This time he wouldn't hesitate at the last moment. He'd take her in his arms and kiss her soundly with his heart on his lips—kiss her as he had never kissed any woman in his life.

He picked up a newspaper and scanned the front page but he scarcely read a single word. The office door opened and he thrust it aside eagerly. Johnny came in and Tony felt a surge of irritated disappointment.

'I wondered where you were,' Johnny said, apparently not noticing anything amiss. He went to the big cupboard in the corner and took out the rounders equipment. 'Some energetic idiots want some exercise,' he said over his shoulder. 'Why on earth did I land the sports side of entertainment in the first place?'

'Consider yourself lucky,' Tony told him without sympathy. 'In fifteen minutes, I've got to handle the Children's Fancy Dress—and that's no joke.'

Johnny laughed. 'Rather you than me, old man. By the way, heard the latest, Tony?

There's a rumour among the staff that Ann's getting engaged to Paul.'

'Paul!' Tony was incredulous. 'But he's a confirmed bachelor since his divorce went through.'

Johnny shrugged and paused by the desk, his arms full of sports gear. 'I'm only passing on gossip. Ann won't say—you know how she loves to be mysterious. Paul isn't available for questioning—he's gone into Midleigh for the afternoon. This engagement business seems to be catching. My only consolation is that I'm not likely to be the next one.'

'Nor me,' Tony replied automatically.

Johnny threw him a quizzical glance. 'Love laughs at the over-confident,' he said. 'Watch your step, Tony!'

As he crossed the ballroom, Gail hailed him and he waited for her to join him.

'Rounders?' he invited as she reached him.

Gail threw him a laughing glance. 'No, thanks—not in this heat. I intend to sunbathe.'

'Have you heard about Ann and Paul?' Johnny asked. 'It seems that they're planning an engagement.'

'Yes, I know. Graham told me,' Gail replied. 'He and Paul are quite friendly and it seems that Paul told him that he was going in to Midleigh to look at engagement rings.'

Johnny pursed his lips. 'I should have thought you'd have known from Ann. She's your chalet-mate, after all.'

'Oh, Ann can be very close when she wishes.'

'What do you think about it?' Johnny asked with interest.

Gail shrugged. 'I'm not sure. Ann's no child—and she's known plenty of men. Of course, Paul is twice her age and he's been divorced—I hope they're really in love otherwise that marriage wouldn't stand a chance.' She indicated the papers in her hand. 'Tony's waiting for these. I'll see you around, Johnny.'

Johnny smiled at her. 'I don't think his impatience is for those lists,' he said cryptically and went on his way before she could question him.

Gail opened the office door and looked in. Tony leaped to his feet. 'Here are your lists, Tony,' she said lightly, handing them to him. He put them down on the table. 'I'm going to do some sunbathing,' she told him and turned to go.

'Gail!' he said urgently.

She paused and looked at him. 'Yes, Tony.'

'Close the door—I want to talk to you,' he said and his lips were dry. She obediently closed the door and leaned against it.

'If you want privacy, you'd better close the window too,' she said lightly, indicating the wide-open casement and the campers who passed at that moment and glanced in, hailing Tony.

He glanced at his watch. 'I've only a few minutes.'

'So have I,' she returned. 'I'm not wasting any more of this glorious sunshine. But you're wasting time and so am I. What is it, Tony?'

He searched her eyes for the faintest trace of encouragement but found none. Her expression was cool and she was completely at her ease. He sought wildly for the right words while she waited, one eyebrow raised in query, a smile lurking at her lips.

'Damn you,' he said lightly. 'You're making it so difficult.'

'You've made things difficult for me for a very long time,' she reminded him. 'Is that what's worrying you? Have you repented of your sins?' She flashed a laughing glance at him. 'Have you decided, after all, that it's better to be friends with me than enemies?' She added quietly and sincerely, 'I hope so, Tony. I can't take much more of it.'

He ran a hand through his dark hair, aware that the time was slipping away, and knowing that he could never hope to impress upon her how sincere he was in his love for her. How could he even put it into words? His eyes were on her face and how gentle, how warm, was her expression. It needed so little for that faint smile to break across her face. It needed one short step to take her into his arms but he lacked the courage, dreading her reactions.

'I regret a great many things,' he told her

stiffly. 'I've hurt you again and again—and that I regret most of all. The things you said about me are quite true—I've been stubborn and conceited and very blind. Gail, can you forgive me? I admit without reserve that I've been a fool.'

Gail's eyes softened. She put out a hand to him and he took it. 'I've not been so intelligent myself—shake hands with another fool.' Her voice shook a little as she tried to speak lightly. 'Please believe that I've only ever wanted your friendship—there hasn't been any thought in my mind of trying to pick up old threads. I realized three years ago that you merely aren't the sort of man to stick to one woman. It hurt at the time—you knew too well how I felt about you then. Well, I got over it—but even the youthful infatuation which you despise so much can be very painful, Tony.'

'Then it was only youthful infatuation?' The words were difficult.

Gail nodded. She hated to resort to lies, but she badly wanted Tony's friendship if she could have nothing else, and if it would ease his mind to know that she no longer loved him, then she would gladly deny the flame which burned just as brightly now in her heart. 'I was very young,' she reminded him unnecessarily.

He smiled at that. 'You aren't very much older now,' he said slowly.

'Oh, I am. Much older and much wiser,' she said and she could not keep the bitterness from her voice.

He dropped her hand and turned to look out of the window. He said quietly: 'The winds of chance—it was totally unexpected that we should meet again here. It seems in a way as though it were planned.'

'Not by me,' she said quickly, afraid. 'I had no idea you worked for Howard.'

'I didn't mean that,' he assured her. 'Planned by whoever it is that plans our lives, Gail. Perhaps there isn't any such thing as chance, after all.' He turned his head and looked at her intently. 'I suppose you wouldn't care to try to pick up the old threads?'

She shook her head swiftly. 'Too much has happened since those days, Tony. I'm not the same impulsive girl—you're still too damn attractive for any woman's peace of mind—but I guess it's like mumps. Once you've got over it, you just don't get it again.'

'Mumps!' Despite his innermost feelings, Tony laughed joyously. She had always had the gift of bringing laughter. Bless her sweet sense of humour! 'Thanks for the compliment,' he said 'back-handed though it was.' He put out his hand and drew her to his side, slipping his arm about her waist. 'You adorable minx!' he said easily and found that all constraint had left him. 'Mumps indeed!'

Gail smiled up at him tremulously. 'It was a bit tactless, I suppose.'

'Don't worry—I needed that laugh,' he told

her. His arm tightened about her. 'Gail, listen to me. And don't interrupt, there's a good girl.' He grinned at her and now triumph was again in his eyes. 'I'm the world's worst imbecile. I waited until you fell out of love with me before realizing that you're the only person I could possibly share my life with—partly because of that sense of humour, partly because you're a trusting little fool'—and this time it was an endearment—'and you need someone like me to protect you from the world, and partly because I love you with all my heart.' He hushed the quick words which sprang to her lips with a fleeting kiss and noted with real joy that her eyes were brighter than they had been for weeks. 'I really mean that, Gail—I do love you. It's taken me a long time to realize it but that doesn't make it any the less true. I've treated you badly—my manners alone have been a disgrace to my parents' strict upbringing.' He grinned again. 'You loved me once. I'm fairly confident that I can win your love again—all I want is the chance to show you that there are better sides to my nature than the ones you've seen. Will you give me that chance?' He waited.

'May I speak now?' she asked with dancing eyes. He nodded. Much as she longed to confess that she had lied, that she had never stopped loving him and that his words had transported her from sadness to rapture, she felt that he deserved a little torment himself and she determined to let him go on thinking that he had to win her love back. 'It's a little hard to believe that you do love me, Tony,' she said slowly and now she was perfectly serious. 'I'm not doubting your word, but it's something that has to be proved. I'm willing to give you the chance to prove it—but I'm not promising that you'll succeed in your aims.' She added hastily: 'Oh, I know that you're very sure of yourself but pride comes before a fall—and I'm not sure that you don't deserve to come a cropper.' Now she smiled, taking the sting from her words. 'It wouldn't be a bad thing for you to lose some of that insufferable conceit—but I suppose you wouldn't be the same irresistible Tony if you did.'

'At least you still think I'm irresistible,' he said.

Gail laughed happily. 'I still think a great many nice things about you—but I've no intention of letting you know what they are. Now, I'm going to lie in the sun and I imagine that you've work to do.'

He sighed. 'You're so right.' He caught her close as she tried to free herself. 'At least let me kiss you before you go, Gail.'

'In full view of any passing camper?' she teased. 'Think of your reputation—mine's in shreds, anyway.'

'To hell with your reputation and mine too,' he retorted and enfolded her in his arms. Hungrily he sought her lips and time stood still as he kissed her, seeking to impart the full force of his love and willingness to make amends for the past. He had never known that the entire world could seem within a man's grasp when he held the woman he loved close to him. His blood was pounding when he finally released her and he knew that without Gail his life would be worth nothing in the future.

Gail did not stop to wonder at the sudden change in Tony's feelings for her. It was too much joy to know that her love was returned in full measure. Every day was welcomed anew with a song in her heart and she lived only for the time she could spend with Tony. She was not naturally a cruel person, so she knew it would not be long that she kept him in suspense. In her heart, she felt sure that he knew how much she loved him but he played up to her deception and did not urge her to confess it.

Johnny could not fail to notice the new spring in her step, the radiant light in her eyes, the happiness which seemed to enfold her entire being. Tony too was a different person. It was impossible that they could keep the warm intimacy of their association from the notice of the staff and campers. It was a subject for comment and some surprise.

It soon came to the ears of Howard and Clare that Gail and Tony were no longer hostile to each other. Clare smiled at Howard.

'I told you they would work it out for themselves,' she said. 'It never pays to interfere, my dear.'

Howard nodded. 'I don't know what germ has hit the camp this year,' he said, 'but it seems to be afflicting one after the other.' Paul and Ann had announced their engagement at the week-end and this had come as a surprise to Howard. He kept his opinions to himself except for discussing the matter with Clare who agreed with him that it would take a deal of co-operation and much love for the marriage to work out—if it ever came off, and who could say that was a certainty when there was such difference in their ages and temperaments.

Johnny smiled at Gail across the table in the cafeteria. Meeting her by the swimming-pool a few minutes earlier, he had invited her to have a cold drink with him and she had accepted gratefully, for the heatwave was continuing. 'So Tony finally came to his senses,' he said lightly. 'Well, I told him often enough to bring his head out of the sand.'

Gail looked at him quickly. 'Then you don't think it was a sudden change of heart?'

'Of course not. Tony was in love with you for weeks—he just couldn't define his own emotions. He didn't like the insecurity and confusion and he preferred to think that he was immune to love, so every time he spoke to you he resented the effect you had on him and turned it into anger and dislike. I've never known him to quarrel with anyone but you—that's proof enough when you know people as well as I do.'

'Quite a student of human nature, aren't you?' Gail teased.

He nodded. 'I get ample opportunities to study it,' he reminded her. He leaned forward and pressed her hand with his own. 'I'm glad things are working out well for you, Gail. It isn't natural for you to be unhappy—you're so high-spirited as a rule.'

Gail grimaced. 'It hasn't been very pleasant at times,' she admitted as memories of past pain and bewilderment flooded back. She studied Johnny's face. She had always sensed his great affection for her. Did he regret that at last she and Tony were likely to find happiness together? It might write *finis* to his own hopes. Impulsively, she asked: 'I'm sorry, Johnny, but you did know long ago that you didn't stand a chance, didn't you?'

He smiled reassuringly. 'Of course I did. I've never tried to hide how I feel about you—but there's no need for you to be sorry for me. I'm just not the marrying type.'

Gail said quietly: 'That's what Tony used to say.'

'Tony? He's been asleep most of his life. I doubt if he had the faintest idea what it was like to be in love with a woman and want to marry her. Perhaps he thought he was immune to love and had no intention of marriage, but that was a defence against his innermost instincts rather than a warning to unattached women to keep off. I don't think you need worry about Tony, my sweet. He thinks you're the beginning and end of the world and no other woman will ever exist for him. I couldn't say the same for myself—that's why I say I'm not the marrying type. I love you, Gail, but I'm not blind to the attractions of other women—I couldn't promise to be if I married you. That isn't a fair proposition to offer any woman.'

'What a really nice person you are, Johnny,' Gail said warmly, sincerely.

He laughed. 'That will probably be my epitaph—still, it isn't a bad recommendation. Now, be sensible, Gail—don't keep Tony waiting much longer. He's like a cat on hot bricks these days—he just doesn't know what to believe about you.'

'Not for the first time,' she retorted. She looked at him curiously. 'How did you know I was keeping him waiting?'

He grinned. 'I know the wicked ways of women. I know a lot and guess the rest—you'd be surprised how right I am in many things.'

Gail took his advice. That same evening, after the dance, they walked together down to the beach. The stars were bright in the heavens. The night was cooler than the day had been. A wind had sprung up and blew Gail's dark curls into her eyes. She had to constantly put up a hand to brush them away. She laughed up at Tony. 'This wouldn't be the wind of chance you were talking about the other day?'

'It was just something that came to me,' he said slowly. 'Watching the smoke from a cigarette—the way it curls in the breeze. I was thinking that our lives are just as helpless against destiny, fortune, chance—call it what you will. We just have to move with the wind— on this path or that—and hope that happiness and not disaster is waiting at the end of it.'

'I certainly never thought that destiny would bring you into my life again,' Gail said thoughtfully.

He drew her close. 'Glad or sorry?'

She put her arms about him and a smile flickered at the edge of her lips. 'Very glad,' she assured him. 'I thought it was a terrible mistake at first when you were so beastly. I suppose even that had a purpose in our lives.'

'Everything has,' he said. 'Your friendship with Graham, for instance. I didn't realize that it would be that which brought home to me that I loved you. I was terribly jealous and so afraid for your trusting innocence because I knew Graham's reputation with women.'

'So unjustified!' she cried. 'He never gave me cause for a single moment to doubt my trust in him.'

'I'm glad of that,' he said and buried his lips against her hair. 'I love you,' he murmured. 'So much, my Gail.'

She caressed his dark head, then turned his face towards her and their lips met in the cool shadow of the night. The stars above looked down benevolently, for they were sympathetic to lovers. The moon sailed out from behind a dark bank of clouds as if to offer its own blessing.

Raising his head, Tony's arms tightened about her, love and desire mingling in his blood. 'Gail,' he whispered urgently. 'I haven't given you much time—but I can't wait any longer. I have to know. Is there any chance that you'll love me again? It means so much to me, my darling.'

She framed his face between her slender, gentle hands. 'All the chance in the world,' she assured him. 'I should have told you before, darling. I lied to you—I've never stopped loving you—or hoping that one day you'd love me. You've always been my whole world to me, Tony.' She sighed a little as the words escaped her. It had been difficult to restrain them so long. 'I felt sure you knew that I loved you?'

He turned his head to kiss her fingertips. 'I knew when it didn't matter to me—when it meant everything, I just didn't know at all how you felt. I guess that's typical of life.'

'Don't talk,' she urged him. 'Just kiss me, my darling.' And he was only too pleased to comply.

X